A KISS FOR GILLIAN

"I'm happy to have been in a position to help you," Avery said awkwardly. "I do not want you to regret marrying me."

"I don't think I regret it." Gillian lifted her eyes to his.

"I don't think I regret it, either."

They were standing too close; he knew it. Their voices had sunk too low, too intimate for so large a space. But the light, fading in a shimmer of dust motes, gave a sense of unreality that freed him. He wasn't Prescott Avery. There was no Jane, Emmet, or Katie. There had never been an Elizabeth. There was only this beautiful woman before him.

He leaned in and kissed her.

It was as though time, which had been slowed down in a still, deep pool, now broke through the dam with a white-water rush. Her response was passionate, urgent. He realized he had only meant to brush her mouth in the kind of kiss he had shared with Elizabeth. But this . . . she was somehow giving and demanding at the same time, and he found he wanted nothing more than to drag her closer and plunge them both deeper into the swirling sensuality of the moment. . . .

Books by Catherine Blair

THE SCANDALOUS MISS DELANEY
THE HERO RETURNS
ATHENA'S CONQUEST
A FAMILY FOR GILLIAN

Published by Zebra Books

A FAMILY FOR GILLIAN

Catherine Blair

ZEBRA BOOKS
KENSINGTON PUBLISHING CORP.
http://www.zebrabooks.com

ZEBRA BOOKS are published by

Kensington Publishing Corp.
850 Third Avenue
New York, NY 10022

All Kensington titles, imprints and distributed lines are available at special quantity discounts for bulk purchases for sales promotion, premiums, fund-raising, educational or institutional use.

Special book excerpts or customized printings can also be created to fit specific needs. For details, write or phone the office of the Kensington Special Sales Manager: Kensington Publishing Corp., 850 Third Avenue, New York, NY 10022. Attn. Special Sales Department. Phone: 1-800-221-2647.

First Printing: October 2001
10 9 8 7 6 5 4 3 2 1

Printed in the United States of America

Chapter One

"I'm going to hate her, you know."

Viscount Prescott Avery looked down at his daughter's grave face and drew a slow breath. "I daresay you'll grow used to her," he said at last.

They would all have to grow used to her.

He wondered again if he had been wise in his decision to remarry. Perhaps he should have waited longer to see if he could not manage the task of raising the children on his own.

He looked down the road, trying to distinguish the form of his future wife's traveling coach through the rain. The streaks of water continued to hiss down with a monotonous and somehow menacing intensity.

Well, it was too late now; the deed was done. He'd offered for the girl sight unseen, and he couldn't very well get out of it now.

"I will not call her Mama." Jane's pale gray eyes narrowed.

He smoothed her hair and shot a helpless glance at his sister, who stood silent and disapproving with baby Kate propped on her hip. He was ashamed to find he was glad Katie's gown covered up her twisted foot. He had written a carefully worded letter to his prospective fiancée mentioning that his youngest daughter was lame, but he found himself reluctant to wish the woman confronted with the fact immediately upon meeting them.

"You will call her whatever she asks to be called," Louisa returned sharply. She fixed Jane with a martial look that even Avery found daunting. For all her severity, his older sister had been good to him since the tragedy. She had offered countless times to take his children in and raise them with her own, but he couldn't give them to someone else to raise, even his closest sister. He didn't want that.

Elizabeth would not have wanted that.

A vision of his fair-haired wife rose up before him. She had been so young, so lovely. . . . He swallowed the bitter urge to curse fate for taking her from him. But his children had spent the last two years without a mother, and there seemed to be no choice but to marry again.

Emmet came bounding down the stairs and into the hallway, where they all stood staring out the open door into the rain. His son was so like Elizabeth. His fair curls and wide, blue eyes made him look innocently pretty, until one saw the flash of devilment in his crooked, five-year-old smile. Avery felt the familiar stab of pain in his chest.

"Is she here yet?" the boy demanded.

"No," Jane replied dolefully. "But her outriders have come. She will be here in a moment. Unless her carriage overturns on the road." She looked rather pleased with the idea.

"I brought her a present," his son announced with a smirk. He held out a jar half-filled with dirty water. A rather desperate-looking fish thrashed about in the confined space.

"She'll probably faint." Jane smiled.

"You will be on your best behavior," Avery reminded them, scowling. "No pranks. Do you hear me?"

Jane rolled her eyes with all the ennui a seven-year-old could muster. She stared into the rain, her chin jutting out beyond her upper lip for a long moment. "You shouldn't replace Mama. We don't need anyone else."

"Don't talk to your father in that tone of voice," Louisa snapped. She might not approve of her brother's remarriage, but she was not going to abet his children in their attempt to sabotage it.

Two years. It hardly seemed as though it had been that long, but of course it had. He had calculated it carefully when he considered offering for Miss Harwell. He needed a mother for his children, and she needed a husband. Desperately.

There was a time when he would have shrugged philosophically when he heard that the daughter of a rich, pompous peer of the realm had been seduced by an actor who then skived off to Italy without a care in the world.

Now, however, they suited each other's needs admirably. Miss Harwell, daughter of his mother's dearest friend from school, immediately required a husband, preferably one far from London. Her family had been all too happy to accept the suit of an unknown widower living in a remote corner of Ireland.

He was beginning to doubt the wisdom of his decision, though. A girl who would allow herself to be seduced would doubtless be naive, if not unbearably stupid. She might spend all her time languishing after her lover rather than raising his children like she ought. He hoped to God she didn't expect *him* to act like some damned Italian actor.

His thoughts were cut short when the traveling coach exploded from the rain with a roar of wheels and a spray of water. Before he had a chance to gather his composure, it had pulled up at the shallow front steps of the house.

He repressed a feeling of irritation when his children pressed themselves to Louisa's skirts and left him to face his new bride alone. Kate began wailing.

The rain-slicked door of the coach opened and a bonnet stepped out. He had the briefest impression that there might be a woman under it before the whole hallway was crowded with wet boxes, trunks and people.

"Merciful heavens!" a shrill voice exclaimed. "The weather! We never have such weather in London. I don't see how you stand it, Lord Avery. If you must live in Ireland, why not Dublin, for heaven's sake? We have traveled the breadth of the country on the worst roads I have ever had the misfortune to see. Really, I might as well have shipped my daughter off to India for all I shall see of her. County Limerick! Honestly, you have as much chance of keeping up with fashion here as you would on the moon."

"We welcome you to Glensharrold House," he said, unable to think of anything else suitable to say. He heard his sister give a derisive snort.

"Ah!" His guest removed her bonnet and examined it with distaste. "Ruined completely. I should have known that something like this would happen in this godforsaken place." Such rain! It's an absolute deluge!"

She gave her suspiciously coal black hair a pat and then drew herself up with a sniff. "Lord Avery, I presume? I am Lady John Harwell and this is Gillian."

A young woman was pushed in front of him. He managed to choke out some kind of greeting, but he was not at all certain what he said. Gillian Harwell was nothing like he had pictured her. Somehow he had envisioned her like Elizabeth, fair and pale, almost ethereal in her fragility. The creature in front of him was a tall, lovely Amazon with frank brown eyes and the wildest head of dark curls he had ever seen.

She smiled with a kind of resigned good humor. "Hello, Lord Avery. Oh my, you look rather alarmed. I imagine I am not quite what you had hoped. Shall I tell the coachman not to bother unhitching the horses?"

"Gillian!" her mother hissed. "Your levity is entirely unbecoming."

Avery looked around at the stunned expressions worn by his sister and children and was inclined to agree with the girl's mother. "I'm delighted you have arrived," he said instead. "This is my sister Lady Louisa Edgecott, and these are my children Jane, Emmet, and Kate." He wished Kate would stop screaming. While he was not at all certain what he thought of Miss Harwell, he did not wish to give her an immediate disgust of his family.

There was something in her robust good looks that made him acutely uncomfortable. It made some kind of sense that if she had been seduced, she must be at least passably attractive, but somehow he wished he had chosen someone more plain. It seemed vaguely disrespectful to Elizabeth to marry a girl who was so striking.

Lady John Harwell bowed stiffly in response to Louisa's glacial smile. Miss Harwell, however, shook his stunned sister warmly by the hand and then turned and did the same to all three of his children. Janie stood stiff as a poker, her mouth a thin line of hate. Emmet giggled uncontrollably and lolled his head around his shoulders in a wiggling dance of embarrassment. Kate stopped squalling and stared at the girl with large round eyes. Her chubby hand reached out for a fistful of frizzy curls.

"Are you to be our new Mama?" Emmet asked loudly, as the girl gently detached herself from Kate's clutches. "Because we don't want—ow!" Louisa's hand tightened into a claw on his shoulder.

"Children," Lady John Harwell said, directing an icy glare at Louisa, "should be seen and not heard."

Avery stifled a feeling of acute misery. Perhaps Miss Harwell would find that she was not quite so desperate to marry after all. He was struck with the sudden suspicion that somehow, in the time since Elizabeth had died, his offspring had become a pack of unmanageable savages.

Emmet dragged his sleeve across his runny nose.

"So!" Avery said brightly. "Would you like to change your clothes before you do anything else? The weather has been quite wretched for days, I'm afraid. I will have tea served in the drawing room in half an hour."

"I will show you to your rooms," Louisa said through tightly clenched teeth.

"Take care with that trunk!" his future mother-in-law snapped. "Do you think I traveled all the way from London just to have all my belongings broken by some ham-handed cretin? It is so hard to find people these days, don't you think, Lady Edgecott? I brought my own maid, of course. She is the only servant I trust with my things. She's temperamental, all the French are, but I would be a sad creature indeed if I hadn't a French maid, wouldn't I?"

She gave Avery a frigid nod and swept regally out of the hallway, her strident voice piercing the house as she criticized her way upstairs.

He loosed a sigh of relief before he realized her daughter was still standing before him.

"Listen," the young woman said urgently, holding up a hand to stop him from speaking. "This doesn't have to happen if you do not wish it. I know I accepted your proposal, and at the time I thought it best, but now I am not at all certain. Oh dear." She winced and then laughed. "That sounded rude. I didn't mean it quite that way. What I mean to say is, I'm not at all convinced that you actually want to marry me."

He swallowed painfully. "Of course I do." It was utterly unthinkable that he should cry off at this point. And one couldn't very well cast her off for being far too young and beautiful. But what if she was one of those young ladies with an incurably romantic disposition? He cursed himself for not marrying the bracket-faced Widow Garth when he had the chance.

Miss Harwell was looking at him with an expression of what could only be deemed suspicion. "I should warn you that my mother will not wish to leave until we are well and truly leg-shackled. However, there is no reason we have to rush anything. It might be best if we waited a bit."

"No, no, there is no need to wait." What if she wanted children of her own? The Widow Garth, twelve years his senior, was known to dislike children, but at least she would not have expected him to sire any more. The idea of fathering children by anyone but Elizabeth did not bear contemplation.

Miss Harwell was watching him with something like sympathetic amusement. "I assure you, you need not worry on my account. It is just, in your letter, you sounded very much as though you wished to have everything settled right away."

He had been rightfully worried that he might change his mind. "Yes. No. Right away. Indeed, I—"

"Gillian!"

"Coming, Mother!" She shot him a conspiratorial grin. "I'll wager you think I'm one of those ninnyhammers who thinks it romantic to marry someone sight unseen." She gave him a consoling pat on the shoulder. "I'm not. I'm afraid I'm shockingly practical. I want to get away from my family, and you want someone to help with yours. I daresay we'll deal famously, once we are used to each other."

"Gillian! My dear, sweet girl. Why are you dawdling?" Her mother's clarion voice was sharp.

She gave him an almost comical look of apology and then darted from the room.

He leaned against the back of the front door in exhaustion. So that was Miss Harwell. The future Lady Avery. Well, she would do as well as anyone. Better than most, actually, since she didn't seem predisposed to fidgets and fancies. He wasn't likely to find anyone else anxious to thrust herself into provincial life with three young children predisposed to dislike her presence and a husband . . . well, a husband who could never love her.

"It's for the children, Elizabeth," he murmured, wandering into the drawing room.

Jane and Emmet had been playing there this morning, and their toys were scattered across the floor. He noticed with a slight cringe that they had elected to tie up Jane's doll and run her over with a miniature cannon.

He swept them up and, for lack of anywhere else to put them, deposited them into the large faux Grecian urn Louisa had given them for Christmas. He had the distinct feeling his sister would approve of neither its use nor his housekeeping habits.

He noted that the vase was becoming rather full of hastily hidden clutter. Perhaps it was best that he marry again. Once more, however, he found himself wishing Miss Harwell was a little bit more on the plain side.

"That woman," Louisa exclaimed, entering the room with a dark expression that left him with little doubt to whom she referred, "is impossible. The blue bedroom wouldn't do for her at all because it faces east, and she can't sleep a wink in the morning, no matter how good the curtains, if her room faces east. The corner room was all wrong, as she thought she might detect a slight draft. In the end there was nothing to do but put her in Elizabeth's room."

She seated herself primly on the sofa. "Oh, don't make that face, Prescott. I had no choice. I know you'd like to make a shrine of it, but you will have to let her daughter sleep there once you marry her." She reached for the bellpull and jerked it rather violently. "And I'm not at all certain you should marry her. What were you thinking? Mama mentioned that there was something havey cavey about her. And willing to marry someone she hadn't even laid eyes on! It strikes me as most odd. If you ask me, she Got Into Trouble." She pronounced the words in capital letters.

"I know what I'm doing, Louisa," he said mildly, hoping it was true.

There was no time for his sister to refute this assertion, as Lady John Harwell swept into the room, followed by his future bride.

He exchanged pleasantries and then duly apologized for the lamentably old-fashioned build of the house, the state of the linen, the prospect from Elizabeth's bedroom window, and the country itself for being so shockingly ill-favored as far as weather, flora, religion, politics, and millinery.

There must be some way out of this engagement. Perhaps he could feign illness. Or madness. It wouldn't tax anyone's mind too much to believe he'd lost his wits.

At least Miss Harwell sat quietly through this exchange, though her face held an expression that was difficult to read.

"I'm sorry to say that your tea is quite inferior to what we get in London." Lady John examined the liquid in her teacup with an expression that suggested she was highly satisfied to make this discovery. "I shall send you a pound from Fortnum and Mason as soon as I return home, Gillian."

"Yes, Mama."

"And you will remember what I said about hiring another nursemaid. One among three children is not nearly enough. Especially when the youngest one is"—her voice dropped to a scandalized whisper—"lame."

He restrained himself with effort. His daughter would suffer enough in life without people like Lady John Harwell to stare at her as though she were a monster.

"I'm certain Lord Avery knows just how to manage his children," Miss Harwell said, serenely stirring her tea.

"After all, it will require special care for the rest of its life—"

"Mother!" she said sharply. "Won't you please pass the sugar?" Her smile was sweet, but pointed. She looked about her, and her face relaxed into a look of more genuine pleasure. "What a pleasant, cozy room this is."

"It is rather small," her mother argued.

"A bit," Avery agreed wearily. Surely it would be understandable if he were to run howling out of the room. Louisa would make the suitable apologies.

"Though I'm certain it is satisfactory in the evenings. If one doesn't entertain," his mother-in-law to be conceded begrudgingly.

He wound up a mechanical smile. "Entirely so."

An uncomfortable silence fell on the room. Rain spattered down the chimney and sizzled on the fire. Louisa sprang up to ring for more tea, though the pot was still halfway full. Avery stifled the acute desire to fling himself out the window.

He cleared his throat. "I obtained a license, so we can dispense with the banns," he said. "We can be married Saturday next."

"Next Saturday? Really, Lord Avery, I don't know how you think Gillian is going to be ready by then! You can't expect a young lady—"

"Next Saturday will be fine," Miss Harwell put in quickly.

Avery rubbed his sweating palms on the knees of

his trousers. "Excellent. We will plan on Saturday then."

"Lovely," Louisa chimed in with a frigid lack of enthusiasm.

Well. It was settled. He had never actually formally proposed to the girl in person, and yet it was somehow all settled. How different this was from how it had been with Elizabeth! He had been only twenty, and she seventeen. The memory of his fumblingly passionate, poetry-filled proposal was somewhat humiliating to recall. But at least it had been a proposal, and not some stilted business arrangement.

"Saturday," Miss Harwell repeated, just to break the silence. Avery resisted the urge to writhe in his chair.

The tea arrived, and he jumped up to relieve the butler of the tray. "Tea!" he announced, with a surfeit of enthusiasm that was painful to hear. "And tea cakes! Would you like a tea cake?"

"Mrs. O'Connor makes lovely tea cakes," Louisa agreed far too heartily.

Lady John Harwell picked one up, examined it critically, and then put it back on the plate. The clock ticking on the mantel seemed suddenly very loud.

Avery took an enormous bite of tea cake. The sound of his chewing seemed to fill the whole room. He swallowed the bolus and cleared his throat. "How long will you be staying?" he croaked.

"Do you hear that?" Miss Harwell asked urgently. Everyone turned to her. "That kind of. . . splashing noise." She cocked her head and listened. Then, to Avery's horror, she picked up the teapot and looked inside. "A fish!" she exclaimed.

"There is a fish in the teapot?" her mother shrieked.

Louisa's eyes met his in alarm. Emmet!

"Miss Harwell, I—"

"Quick! Quick!" Miss Harwell leaped up with the teapot and looked around wildly. She spied a vase of flowers, and before anyone could stop her, she had thrown the blooms on the floor, reached her hand into the teapot, and transferred the fish into the water.

She stood for a moment peering into the vase. "There. I think it will be all right." She looked somewhat surprised to see everyone in the room staring at her in dismay. "Well, I daresay it can't be good for a fish to live in a pot of tea," she said defensively.

"No," Avery choked. "Most likely not." He had expected Miss Harwell to be plain, he had expected her to be naive, he had expected her to be chastened by the recent debacle of her seduction. But now he had the feeling that the second Lady Avery was going to be nothing like what he had expected.

Chapter Two

Gillian was certain she had descended into the seventh circle of hell. It had been a while since she had read Dante's *Inferno,* but surely there was one level filled with nothing but screaming children. She detached one from her skirt, noted the jam-colored decorations it left behind, and watched in dismay as it tottered, fell face first onto the carpet, and began howling.

"Now you see what you've gotten yourself into," her mother hissed with a kind of irritated satisfaction. "Married to a provincial nobody with a pack of children. My grandchildren will never be heirs to anything."

Gillian set the child on its feet and watched it wend its way through the perilous crowd of legs that made up the wedding breakfast guests. She stood up and looked her mother in the eye. "I suppose not," she said.

"I had both Lord Winn and Lord Stubblefield on the very brink of offering for you, and you had to go and ruin yourself."

"I told you, I did not wish to marry any of the men you had collected for me," she reminded her. It was ridiculous to be having this argument again. As of two hours ago, when she and Avery had signed the church registry, the question of who should marry had been settled.

Lady John Harwell carefully held her skirts away from two little girls who ran screeching through the crowd, armed with sticky buns. "At least I managed to get you respectably settled despite yourself," she sniffed. "Even if you are at the ends of the earth. I suppose it is best, as no one of good ton in London would have opened their door to you anyway. Really, Gillian, you are lucky you were not thrust out upon the street. It is what most families would have done, I assure you."

"Undoubtedly." It would have been preferable to marriage to any of her mother's choices, in any case. A curly-haired baby who had been happily beating a spoon against the table leg now took it upon himself to launch his body toward her. Gillian caught him up just before the spoon became painfully imbedded between the two of them.

"That's Sarah's fourth, little Horatio," a woman nearby provided with a smile. "He is only fourteen months. Of course, my Josephine was walking at ten and certainly knows a great many more words at eighteen months than either Horatio or Francis, Ellen's boy. But of course girls are so much quicker than boys."

"Oh yes," Gillian agreed with a vigorous nod, hoping it made her look knowledgeable about such things. "And Ellen is?"

"Ellen, Sarah, George, John, Jane, and myself are all Daltons. Cousins to Prescott," she added, with a look that suggested Gillian was more than a little dull-witted not to have known all this.

It took her a moment to remember that Prescott was Lord Avery's Christian name. She racked her brains. Was this cousin Mary? Marianne? She was never going to get everyone straight. Especially when none of them ever seemed to stop talking and running about.

"Sarah is married to John Willis, and Jane is married to that man over there, John Dunne. Our brother John also married a Sarah, which makes things very confusing indeed."

"Indeed." Gillian gave a feeble laugh. She struggled to catch a glimpse of her husband through the crowd.

Her husband. Married. She took another sip of negus and tried not to contemplate the enormity of what had just happened.

"Prescott's sister Louisa is married to the man over there in the green coat. He is an Edgecott from Clare. Their children are William, Reginald, Fiona, and George," the woman explained.

"I thought that was George." She pointed to a man looking miserably trapped in conversation with her mother.

Avery's cousin laughed. "It is. But Louisa has a little George. Actually, so does Jane. Jane Dalton, I mean, of course, not Prescott's daughter. Come to think on it, Ellen has a George, too."

"So should we all," Gillian muttered.

"Marianne, you are beginning to sound like Deuteronomy." Avery approached them, smiling. "You will have poor Miss Harwell's head spinning if you try to explain it all to her now." He stooped to removed a fork from a child who was doing his best to perforate himself. "She cannot be used to all this hubbub."

"She is not Miss Harwell. She is Lady Avery," Marianne reminded him, smiling archly.

Gillian saw the tips of his ears turn pink. "Yes, of course. Takes a bit of getting used to. Lady Avery. Of course." The words seemed to stick in his throat.

"It is a bit odd, isn't it?" she said with a sympathetic laugh. It was more than a bit odd. Married and away from her family forever. She might have felt relieved if it weren't for the rather sickly feeling in her stomach. Married to the stranger beside her forever.

Avery raised his voice over the noise. "I know this must seem like a complete melee to you, but our family gatherings are always this way. We are very close and, as you can see, very voluble." A group of young people were busily stripping the room of furniture so they could roll up the rugs and dance. It occurred to her it was now her house, her furniture, and her rugs, but it hardly seemed that way. It was all so terribly foreign.

Someone's child had tipped the cream pitcher over his head and was wailing. Avery picked the child up and carried it with him like a curiosity as they continued on their circuit of the room.

"Gatherings like these are amongst my happiest memories," he said with a smile. "But you are an only child. How strange it must all be to you."

"Yes. I suppose it is." It did not seem polite to admit to a blinding headache. She saw her mother gesturing frantically for her, but pretended not to. "I'm very glad we decided not to wait," she said fervently. Any man who would forgive her the sin of being ruined would certainly forgive the little deception she had forged. Surely.

Her mother was cutting her way through the crowd toward her. Gillian took Avery by the elbow and pulled him into the next room. He looked bewildered by this show of force, but merely took up a napkin from the table nearby and began drying the cream from his young charge's hair. He then set the boy on his feet, but he immediately fell down, dragging the tablecloth and several dishes down upon him.

"One of the Georges?" Gillian asked weakly.

"One of the Georges."

She looked around for Avery's children in the crowd. There was Jane, squashed in a chair with another little girl the same age. They were giggling together and sharing an enormous piece of wedding cake. She hardly looked like the same girl who had spent the best part of the last week in a sulk and had nearly been banned from the wedding for fear she might make a scene.

"Papa!" A boy came running up and threw himself at Avery's knees. Gillian was relieved to recognize this child as Emmet.

"I want another piece of cake, but Jane said I mightn't. I said she was stupid. Can I have one?"

Avery opened his mouth and then closed it. He appeared to struggle for a moment. "You'll have to ask ... ask your Mama." He closed his eyes before he said the word.

Emmet was wearing the same expression of wary confusion she was. "Mama?" His pale brows lowered dangerously.

"Oh, please, they don't have to call me that. In fact, I really would rather—"

"I won't call her Mama!" Emmet shouted. "I won't! I won't!"

It was one of those moments where the whole room had a collective lull in conversation. Emmet might as well have roared through a speaking trumpet.

Avery's jaw tensed. "Emmet, you will do as I say. I will not have you speak disrespectfully to Miss Ha—to Gillian."

She wasn't even aware he knew her Christian name. He had certainly never used it. His West Limerick accent gave it a whole different sound. It was rather nice.

She crouched down to Emmet's level. "Perhaps we can think of a different name you would like to call me," she said in her best placating tone.

Emmet looked at her, his blue eyes steeped in tears. "Stupid!" he shouted. "I want to call you stupid, stupid, stupid-head!"

The entire world stared at them in scandalized horror. Avery drew a tight breath of fury.

"That's a bit of a long name," Gillian said mildly. "Perhaps you could abbreviate it to something shorter. Stu, perhaps."

Emmet blinked once and stared at her. Then a giggle bubbled out of him like a belch.

"Emmet!" Jane hissed, bearing down upon her brother like an angry goose. "Don't laugh at her. Don't talk to her." She started to drag him away, but Avery caught her by the shoulder.

"Jane, Emmet, you will not behave in such a ramshackle manner. Look at Aunt Louisa's children. Aren't they well behaved?" There was a pleading tone in his voice.

Gillian looked at where Louisa's children sat in a row in descending order of size on the couch.

"They would never be so horrid to . . . to their new stepmother," Avery prompted.

"Yes, they would," Emmet said boldly, "if they had one."

"Emmet!" Her husband's voice was sharp. "Apologize to Gillian for being rude."

The little boy's mouth pinched into a small, red knot. " 'Pologize," he grunted at last.

The two children stood at attention for a moment and then dashed away.

"I'm sorry for that," Avery said in a low voice.

"Oh, it is nôt surprising." Gillian shrugged. It was ridiculous that she should feel humiliated by a five-year-old boy. "They've had very little time to get used to the notion." Her eyes met his. "Neither have we."

Avery guided her to a chair and sat down next to her, his hands awkwardly on his knees. He smiled stiffly, and she smiled back. He cleared his throat.

"I'm sorry the weather was not better for the wedding. Of course, every Irish county claims to be the wettest, but I have no personal doubt Limerick holds the title.

"They say it is good luck if it rains on your wedding day, but I suspect it is merely said to console the bride." Her laugh sounded forced, even to her own ears. Dear God, married half a day and they were reduced to talking about the weather. If she smiled any more, her cheeks would burst open like ripe plums.

He examined the ceiling as though it were the sky. "It dates back to pagan times. Rain is a symbol of fertility."

Fertility. Fertility required the marriage act. He must have had the same thought as she did, for there was a sudden flush on his cheekbones.

"Lots of pagan customs still around," he continued in a rush. "All the major Christian holidays are based around them."

Would her new husband wish to consummate the marriage? Tonight? Of course, as she was considered ruined, he would feel no need to woo her as he would a virgin bride.

Perhaps it would not be so very terrible. He was handsome—very handsome, really. His sky blue eyes would have been devastating if there was a spark of humor in them instead of the perpetual patina of worry. His dark curls fell rakishly over one brow, but that brow was nearly always creased.

". . . All Hallow's Eve, of course, has roots in many civilizations and is based in ancestor worship," he continued. "While we are sadly lacking in them here, there is a fine pagan burial site north of Dublin. It is an enormous mound with a very narrow passage to a central chamber. Very like the chamber tombs found in Egyptian pyramids."

"Indeed?" She would have to tell him at some point. It might have been better to have included him in on the deception at the start. At least then if he did, perhaps, have the desire to bed her, he would know she was innocent after all. Would he be annoyed? Relieved?

". . . St. Steven's day is very much based on the winter solstice. I've always been curious how it managed to retain its separate identity from Christmas. Why they are celebrated a day apart when they are rooted in the same holiday is a bit of a mystery. I suspect the early church thought it best to retain a day of feasting and music that is basically highly secular, despite its saint's name."

"Oh, yes." She nodded inanely. "I know just

what you mean.'' Perhaps, as he already had an heir, he would not wish to touch her at all.

''. . . And of course St. Valentine's Day is merely another pagan holiday given over to a saint. All the love poems and romantic nonsense are veneer over a fertility festival. Oh dear.'' He looked slightly sheepish. ''We seem to have come back to that subject again.''

''Yes,'' she said, sighing. ''I suppose it all does come back to that.''

Chapter Three

"I do hate to leave you here in this dreadful place among strangers." Her mother tied on her bonnet and looked out into the rain with distaste. "Not that it isn't your own fault, of course. Really, Gillian, I don't know how I am going to face the sneers of Mrs. Woodcock and Lady Delling. At least I got you respectably married. I thought until the last that you would say you would not have it. The way you carry on, one would think you didn't wish to be married at all."

Gillian listened for the horses coming around to the front of the house. "Well, I am now, aren't I?" she said, her smile firm. "Give my regards to Papa, of course."

"I'll write you with advice on engaging another nursemaid. And, really, you must get rid of that housekeeper. She thinks she runs the place entirely. You'll get no peace with her here."

"Thank you, Mama. I look forward to your letters." The coachman seemed to be forever about letting down the steps. She gave her mother a kiss on the cheek. "I'm sorry I've been a disappointment to you."

Lady John pulled her cloak closer together at the neck and gave a low moan. "When I think of the brilliant match you might have made, I could cry. I really could. Lord Winn *and* Lord Stubblefield ready to offer! And you had to—"

"Oh dear, the coach is ready to go. Don't keep them waiting, Mama. The weather is truly dreadful." She looked up and saw Lord Avery come out of his study.

He came to them and bowed politely over her mother's hand. "I hope you have a good journey," he said.

"With these roads? I'll be lucky if the carriage doesn't get stuck in the drive. It will likely take me a month to get to Dublin and then the passage . . . ." Her expression left no doubt as to her emotions.

"Good-bye, Mama," Gillian said cheerfully. "Thank you for accompanying me here."

"I shall likely die of sea sickness. I never saw such waves. And I will be amazed if your father remembers what ship I am on or what day I am arriving back. I will likely have to spend a night in Holyhead, and you know there isn't an inn in the town with sheets that aren't damp."

"Good-bye." She waved her mother into the rain.

"Thank you for bringing me Gillian," Avery called out. "I will take care of her."

For some reason the words made her insides ache. He would take care of her. What a kind thing to say. But she had known from his letter he would be kind. She had never found the chance to tell him how much it had meant to her. In a single sheet of paper, he had made her feel there was someone in the world who might understand her, a kind of kindred soul in the world. It sounded ridiculously fanciful, something she prided herself in not being, but reading that letter, she had known she could marry him.

As the coach drove off, she turned to her husband to thank him. But the study door had already closed on his heels.

She frowned for a moment, then walked back to the kitchen where she had been helping Mrs. O'Connor. How annoying that she would be hurt by his remoteness. How could one be hurt by someone one didn't know?

She picked up her spoon and leaned an elbow on the table. It would be nice to have as much solitude as she wished. She could have the privacy she had always craved, with no one at her shoulder haranguing her to sit up straight and smile if she ever wanted to catch a husband. She already had one.

Though she wasn't absolutely positive he really counted as one. She picked up the bowl of whipping cream and began thrashing it again. If they hadn't consummated the marriage, was it still official?

It nearly made her laugh to think about how worried she had been about it last night. She had somehow thought he would pounce on her the moment the wedding guests had gone home. Instead, he had gone upstairs to see that the children were tucked into bed, and she had not seen him again.

"Stupid, stupid, stupid-head," she muttered into the bowl.

Even today he had risen before her, gone for a long ride, and then cloistered himself in his study with the estate manager. Except for that brief moment when he bid her mother good-bye, she had not seen him at all. It was a rather depressing start to a marriage, even one that was made entirely for convenience.

Avery did not want a wife. He wanted a mother for his children, yet so far he hadn't even let her act in that capacity. Her hand paused for a moment. She wasn't even certain she knew how to be a nursemaid, when it came right down to it. But surely it was something that came naturally. After all, nature would not have made one capable of bearing children if it did not give one some innate knowledge of how to take care of them.

"Well, it would have been right of him to have warned me he didn't mean to bed me. At least then I would not have spent half the evening in fits of anxiety over it." She went back to work on the white froth.

"Milady!" Mrs. O'Connor looked over in alarm. "I needed whipped cream. You've nearly made butter. We'll have to start again."

"Oh, dear. Sorry." She put down the bowl and wiped her hands on her apron. "I suppose I am not being much help."

The cook poked at the stiff mass in the bowl with a spoon and gave a faint sigh of disappointment. "If you want to be a help, you could decide on the week's menu. That's what the first Lady Avery always did on a Sunday."

"Oh. Well, I suppose I had better do that." Though her hands were clean, she wiped them again, trying to remember if she had ever actually planned a menu before. Elizabeth, of course, had probably been perfectly able to both whip cream and make menus. She felt a vague sense of sympathy for Avery, who would soon discover his new wife was somewhat impaired in the culinary arena.

"Remember, Lord Avery doesn't like turnips. He'll eat lamb, but not mutton. And there's nothing he likes better than my roast pheasant. Miss Jane likes a nice meat pie and insists on cake for dessert every night, but she can't abide preserves. Master Emmet likes preserves but not cake, and he won't eat anything dairy. He just won't. He's not keen on anything brown, either, but we're working on it."

"And the baby?" Gillian asked in a dry tone.

The woman threw up her hands in a gesture of frustration. "The baby won't eat anything but my special bread pudding. So don't you go trying to force anything fancy on her. She won't eat it."

An hour and a quarter later, Gillian came to the frustrated conclusion that it was impossible to formulate a nonmutton, nonpreserve, nondairy, non*brown* menu. She carefully fished a wooden disk from Emmet's draughts game out of the inkwell and then sighed. If the first Lady Avery had managed such a convoluted piece of menu-making strategy, her family must have been the most malnourished in the county. She frowned up at the ceiling, where she could hear muffled shrieks and bumps from the direction of the nursery.

She threw down her pen and crossed her arms. Well, things would have to change. Avery couldn't very well marry her and expect her to stay out of the way and make things just as they had been when his first wife was alive. There would have to be some changes.

Of course, she wasn't absolutely certain she wanted to admit that she knew very little about how to run a household. Unfortunately, her mother's training had run much more in the line of how to get a husband, not what to do once one had one—much less one with three very noisy children.

The screaming was louder now, and the thumps more frenzied. There was a crash and then stillness.

"What is going on?" she demanded, running up the stairs and bursting into the nursery.

Three pairs of eyes looked up at her with startled expressions. One pair belonged to the nursemaid, who lay bound and gagged on the floor. Jane and Emmet looked painfully innocent.

"We were playing pirates," Jane announced, her chin up. "And Bitsy was our captive."

"She likes to be the captive," Emmet assured her.

Bitsy's clumsy writhing suggested that this might not precisely represent her feelings on the subject.

"Well, I am the captain of another ship, come to rescue her." Gillian knelt down and untied the poor girl. How had the silly creature managed to get herself into such a mess?

"I asked for quarter! Really, milady, I did," she panted, staggering to her feet.

"Well, you should have known these bloodthirsty pirates never would have given it." Gillian could not help smiling at the children, belligerent in their battered cocked hats and wooden swords.

"I'm the gunner," Emmet announced, undaunted by his captive's escape. "And Katie was our bo'sun, but she cried when I shot her with my cannon.'' He pointed at a miniature cannon perched on the head of his bed.

"It was an accident!" he protested when his sister elbowed him. "And she wasn't a good bo'sun anyhow, because she fell asleep." He indicated where Katie lay, placidly sucking her thumb, on a pile of tin doubloons. Her cocked hat was tilted rakishly over one eye.

"Well, your prisoner has escaped, and I don't think there will be any more captive-taking today. After all, you might be near a tropical island where you could stop for the night and have some of the delicious monkey meat pie the cook has prepared for you."

"Monkey meat?" Emmet looked intrigued.

"We are not Caribbean pirates," Jane said in the aloof voice of a duchess. "We're French privateers off the coast of Brest." She looked at Gillian as though she were pathetically dull-witted.

"We might have met some Caribbean pirates and *traded* for some monkey meat pies," Emmet suggested hopefully.

"Well, perhaps you French privateers would consider making a small coastal raid on the kitchen of an unsuspecting nobleman," Gillian said in French.

"Papa said I don't have to start learning French until next year." Jane rolled her eyes with a bored expression. "And it is very rude to speak it when we don't understand it."

"I said—"

"We don't want you to play with us, Stepmother." The girl emphasized the "step" with a narrow-eyed deliberateness.

Emmet scratched his ear. "We might, if she knew

lots of stories about eating monkey meat. And cannibals. Do you know any stories about cannibals?"

"Jane, I don't appreciate that tone in your voice," Gillian said sharply. She resisted the urge to wince, hearing herself say the words her mother had used thousands of times when she was growing up.

Bitsy, sensing a squall was in the air, swept up Katie and bore her off to the girls' bedroom.

Jane crossed her arms and looked insolently up at Gillian. Emmet scowled and jabbed his wooden sword into the toe of his shoe.

She sat down in a small chair and clasped her hands. The chair was evidently meant to represent the bow of the boat, since it had a doll tied to it as a figurehead. "Now, I know it is difficult having a stranger move into the house and having her start telling you what to do."

Emmet and Jane stared at her, unresponsive.

"And I know it will take a while before everything settles down to normal."

Jane's mouth pinched into a thin, white line. "My mother is dead. There is no more normal."

Gillian felt a wash of pity for the children. But still, if she didn't assert her authority now . . . "I know that. But it would be best if you didn't tie up Bitsy any more. Perhaps you could use one of your dolls as a captive instead."

"They don't yell or anything," Emmet muttered in disgust.

Jane continued to look at her as though she was extremely stupid.

"And we should all strive to treat each other with civility. I will make allowances for the newness of the situation, and you must make an effort to grow used to it." What did she think she was doing, making silly, stilted speeches like that? She sounded like she was talking to parliament, not two young children.

"Well," she said, slapping her hands to her knees. "Let's do something fun. Shall we read a book together?"

Although her own enthusiasm made her want to roll her eyes, she was annoyed to see the children actually do so.

"I'd rather not," Jane said. The careful politeness in her voice was oppressive.

"I'd rather not, too," Emmet echoed. "Let's go sail my boat in the stream. We can play pirates with that."

"But it is raining! Is the stream dangerous? Does your father let you do that?" She was suddenly struck with the rather awful notion that she was responsible not only for raising these sprogs to be upstanding, relatively noncriminal members of society, but assuring that they lived to adulthood in the first place.

The door swung open and Avery stuck his head in.

"Is everything all right?" he asked. When he saw Gillian, a tiny frown of worry formed between his brows.

"Papa!" both of the children shouted in unison. They danced across the room and threw themselves into his arms.

"I thought I heard an awful lot of noise up here."

"We were just playing pirates with Bitsy," Jane said sweetly. "But Stepmother made us stop."

Avery looked up, concerned. "Was the noise bothering you?"

"No, not at all, it's just . . ." She felt guilty telling

tales on the children. "Bitsy didn't seem to want to play anymore." She felt like a complete fool.

He looked fondly down at his children. "Well, we must be kind to Bitsy. She has a great deal to put up with in taking care of you."

"Stepmother said we couldn't play anymore," Emmet said sulkily. "And then she said she was going to make us eat monkey meat."

"I didn't!" Gillian felt like she herself was five years old. But at least if she was, she wouldn't feel as though it was impossible to defend herself. She couldn't very well tell her husband of two days that his children were lying to him.

"Monkey meat?" One dark eyebrow quirked upward. "I'm certain she was joking."

Something in his expression was mildly censorious, and it stung. Well, what did he expect her to do when his children were spoilt little monsters? She cursed Bitsy for not being there to defend her.

"Yes," she said, smiling weakly. "I was joking."

"Will you play by the stream with us, Papa? We were going to float the boat you gave me." Emmet tugged at his father's coat.

"Of course I will." He squatted down and smiled down at them with an expression that caught strangely in Gillian's chest. "In fact, why don't we go and ask Mrs. O'Connor to pack up a little luncheon for us, and we will walk down to the pond. The stream will only wash your boat away. On the pond we can have a real sea adventure."

The children clung to him as he continued to expand on their wild adventures on the ocean. Gillian stood where she was, feeling strangely left out.

"I'll go and ask Mrs. O'Connor for the luncheon,

and then we can all go," she suggested, forcing a hopeful smile.

Avery looked up as though he had forgotten she was there. "Oh. Gillian. Are you certain you would enjoy yourself?" He looked hesitant. "The children can be a little boisterous."

"Papa." Emmet looked at his father with a pleading expression. "I want it to be just us. Can't it please be just us?"

"Well, I think it would be nice if we could include your stepmother."

He didn't sound very convincing. Very well. She couldn't force herself into their little group, and there was little point in letting it hurt her. She felt a sudden and very unexpected longing to be looked at with the complete adoration the children gave Avery. But how ridiculous. She, who had been willing to give anything to have her independence, did not need people to fawn on her.

"I just remembered I have some very important things to do," she said in a voice so bright it might have been deemed sarcastic.

"Next time, Gillian." His voice was low and apologetic.

"No, no don't worry about me. I have to see to dinner." She brushed past them with an airy gesture.

"What is for dinner?" Emmet demanded.

Gillian looked back with an expression of supreme sweetness. "Monkey meat."

Chapter Four

It had been a terrible idea. Avery walked through the drizzle toward the house chastising himself. Emmet had, of course, managed to fall into the pond and was wet, muddy, and crying. Jane was complaining grievously because her brother's clumsiness had cut short their playtime.

And Avery felt guilty.

He should have insisted Gillian come with them. It would have been the polite thing to do. If she had been a guest he would have done so. And she wasn't a guest. She was his wife.

"Look," he said, cutting off Janie's monologue of the wrongs done her. "Here is Bitsy come to take you in. Make certain you lay out your oilskins before the fire so that they dry. Janie, be a dear and take the boat back up to the nursery."

He deposited the soggy Emmet into the nurse-maid's arms and loped up the stairs. He noticed with a faint feeling of surprise that they were singularly free of the toys that usually ensured at least one brush with death during his ascent. He'd better make amends with Gillian right away. It was unfortunate that they had gotten off on the wrong foot. He certainly could have done a better job of welcoming her to the family. But, well, dash it all, he didn't even know the woman.

But, his conscience reminded him, he had married her, and no matter what he thought of that decision now, he had to be, well, at least polite.

He looked in the study, the drawing room, her private sitting room. No Gillian. He wondered if she was the type of woman who would go off to sulk.

The girl he had asked to act as her maid was sitting on the bedroom floor carefully folding up some linen. She dropped her hands to her lap and looked slightly embarrassed. He could see she was holding a shift.

"Have you seen Lady Avery?" he asked. It was likely the only glimpse he would ever get of his wife's underclothes. The idea made him smile. Well, so be it. He had made the decision to stay away from her.

The girl continued to stare at him with a mortified expression. "I think she went off riding, milord," she stammered.

"Was she . . . was she in a temper?" He felt ridiculous for asking the question.

"I couldn't say, milord."

"When do you expect her back?"

The girl only wadded the shift in her lap and blushed deeper. "I don't rightly know, milord."

He hoped his wife was nothing like her mother when she was in a temper. He sighed and tromped out toward the stables, feeling more annoyed than contrite.

"Gillian?"

Why had he gotten the stupid notion in his head that he needed to remarry? The children weren't ready. He wasn't ready.

There was no response. Her horse was in its stall, but it looked recently curried. One of the grooms jerked his head in the direction of the feed room. There was a strange creaking sound coming from inside.

For some reason the sound was familiar, but he couldn't remember what it was. He cautiously peered around the door.

It was the swing. He had forgotten about it. It was something he and his brothers had rigged up when they were children and had played on for hours in the long summer afternoons.

Gillian swung back and forth, in and out of a shaft of watery winter sunlight that filtered in from the single, high window near the roof. The ropes creaked as they shifted on the rafters, but he knew they were sturdy. He and Janie used to play here when Emmet was tiny and Katie not yet born. But they hadn't come here since Elizabeth died.

Gillian leaned further back to make the swing go higher. Her dress fluttered like the wings of the disturbed sparrows who had made little nests in the eaves. They occasionally darted down to voice their objection to her presence. She swooped back and forth, higher and higher, until her slippers nearly touched the loft that jutted out along the opposite wall.

She was laughing like a maniac.

There was something entirely uninhibited in her

laugh that made him want to laugh, too. When her head jerked up in alarm, he realized he had.

"I didn't hear you come in," she said, vainly trying to stop the swing.

"You don't have to stop. I just wondered where you were." He wondered if she wanted him to withdraw, but he was curiously unable to do so. He pretended not to notice the remarkable stretch of leg she was exposing.

Her wild curls had escaped from their careful coif and were springing up all over her head. The shaft of sun from the high windows lit up the blond hairs among the chestnut ones and gave her a golden corona like a Byzantine madonna.

She dragged her toes until the swing slowed. Little clouds of hay spun up into the dusty air with each sweep. "Well, I saw the swing here, and I couldn't resist giving it a go." She looked a little embarrassed.

"I used to play here often as a boy. My brothers and I rigged the swing and used to stage daring contests to see who could jump out when it was swinging the highest. William broke his wrist here when he was twelve, and I my collarbone when I was thirteen." He waded toward her through the drifts of loose hay on the floor. "You should be careful out here, though. I believe there are rats among the stores."

"Not anymore," she smiled up at him. "Healy has brought in a family of cats. You are no longer overrun with rats." The trembling corners of her lips tried unsuccessfully to contain a laugh. "You are overrun with kittens."

Avery felt the same pull of desire he had experienced when he first met her. He frowned. "Why are you out here by yourself?"

His voice was gruffer than he had meant for it to be, but he was suddenly aware that they were alone. It occurred to him with a tingling of panic that they had never been alone before.

She smiled, innocently unaware of the thoughts he was struggling to repress. "I am merely amusing myself. I didn't come out here in a pet, if that is what you are thinking."

He took hold of one of the ropes of the swing and leaned his head against his hand. "Gillian, I need to apologize to you. My whole family needs to apologize to you. I have grown very indulgent of the children, and they have not benefited by it. I should have made them invite you along on our outing."

Her eyes did not meet his. "It doesn't matter."

There was a long silence. He knew he should move away, but he did not. He watched her fingers as she pulled at the fibers of the rope below his hand.

"Your children are very attached to you. It is easy to see how much they adore you," she said.

He stilled her hands by kneeling down beside her and covering them with his own. "They will adore you, too. They just need time."

Her smile was sad. "You all need time."

He drew a breath, looked up at her, and finding her dark eyes too intently upon him, turned away. "Yes." He noticed with some alarm that his thumb was stroking the back of her hand, and he removed it quickly. She did not appear to have noticed.

"I know I have put you in a difficult situation, Gillian. This is all so new for you. My family must seem very overwhelming and my children . . . well, they have become very willful since . . . since Elizabeth died."

He felt like his throat was closing up. "My family is so close. You have seen us. We all live in each other's pockets. I was fortunate enough to have had a happy childhood, with parents who loved each other. I want that for my own children."

"Well," she said with a bemused expression, "having known you for only a short time, I cannot honestly say that I love you, but I will do everything I can to keep your children happy."

He rubbed his hands over his face to cover his discomfort. "I didn't mean you had to pretend to be in love with me. That is ... I just ... I just wanted to give my children a mother."

"And that is all," she said calmly, twisting slightly in the swing.

Dear God, but she was blunt. "Oh, well, I didn't mean that precisely. That is ..." Just the thought brought on a shameful wash of desire.

He had deliberately avoided thinking about that aspect of remarriage. He had assumed normal marital relations would be a part of it, of course, but that was before he had known Gillian had the smooth, soft skin of a hothouse peach and the most fascinating amber-brown eyes seen by man. It was before he had known he would want to bed her every time he saw her. And somehow that made all the difference.

"I understand." There was a tone of resignation in her voice. "I am ruined. And the idea of having another man's leavings is repugnant to you."

She stood up and took a step back to start the swing again, but Avery stepped into her path. "That isn't it at all."

They stood for a moment, face to face, saying nothing. "Do you grieve over his going?" he asked quietly at last.

She stared at him for a moment, her head cocked like a little bird. "Can I tell you my secret?" she asked, looking up at him with those guileless eyes.

Dear God. Now she was going to tell him the sordid details of her seduction. A thought struck him in the stomach—was she with child?

It shouldn't bother him. He had an heir, and another child in the house would make no difference. He should have expected it from the start when she accepted his unexpected proposal with such alacrity. And he himself certainly wasn't going to have children by her. Her child would complete the appearance that their sham marriage was everything it should be. He stifled the unreasonable sense of anger. "Of course," he said calmly.

She leaned back in the swing and looked at the ceiling for a moment. Then she looked him in the face. "I'm not actually ruined."

"What?"

She shrugged, her expression almost sheepish. "Mama had high hopes for my marriage, and nothing would make her believe that I had no desire for it. The men she had brought up to scratch, as the vulgar expression is, were men I could not only never love, but never respect or even stand to be in the same room with. Utterly dissolute." To his dismay, she laughed. "I know you will think I exaggerate, but you really must believe they were utterly unsuitable."

He stared at her in bewilderment. "Then why—"

"You've met my mother," she said with a rueful expression. "Once she sets her teeth in a notion, there is no calling her off it." Her toes on the ground, she pivoted the swing back and forth. "I conceived of a plan to ruin myself. That way no one would wish to marry me. And if I was very lucky"—again she laughed—"I should be sent away from my family forever."

"You aren't ruined." He felt a slightly hysterical laugh welling up within him.

"My cousin had a friend who was an actor," she continued. "He contrived to introduce us, and I contrived that we should be seen together on several occasions." Her eyes twinkled. "I will never forget the last night we spent together, staring across the table at each other at some wretched tavern or other, bored out of our heads. After it was shockingly late, I gave James enough money to hie off to Italy, and I hired a hack to take me home."

"Not ruined," he repeated, dully.

She wrinkled her nose. "Well, my reputation was ruined, in any case, and apparently that is what matters."

"Then why—" It made no sense to him. How could she possibly have been so desperate to escape marriage that she would throw away the only thing that made her respectable to society? The fact that he was married to a woman as opposed to the institution as he himself was not as comforting as it should have been.

She heaved a sympathetic sigh. "Oh, dear, you really have been hoaxed, haven't you? I'm so sorry. I should have told you from the first. But you see, I never intended to marry you. Or anyone. I daresay I wouldn't have had to do anything if your letter hadn't arrived."

The letter. How well he remembered writing it. He must have gone through seven drafts, at least. How could one write a stranger and propose a shockingly businesslike alliance, alluding to the fact that he knew she was sullied, but did not mind?

It had been dashed awkward. He had very nearly not sent it at all. Only his slight pity for the poor unknown ruined girl had strengthened his resolve. And now she claimed she wasn't ruined at all.

"It was very kind." There was a warmth in her eyes that made him feel suddenly uncomfortable. "You were so polite, and you sounded so very, well, so very gentle. Not in the least bit pompous or stuffy. Of course Mama, knowing I would never get another offer, was not about to let me refuse you, but I didn't mind so very much." She put her hand on his sleeve and smiled up at him. "It was a very kind letter," she repeated.

They were standing far too close. He could see how her lashes were tangled at the corners. He dragged his eyes away.

"So there you are," she said in a cheery voice that seemed to cover sadness. "Hoist by my own petard."

He felt a novel sense of admiration for a woman who had gone to such lengths to take control of her own life. But here she was, trapped in the very kind of loveless marriage she had been trying to avoid. He noticed that, again, his hand had somehow come to cover her own, but this time he could not bring himself to remove it.

Her peculiar, tea-colored eyes were upon him. "I don't mean for it to sound like I think my life here is punishment for my mistakes," she said in a low voice that was suddenly serious. "It sounds dreadful, but my main hope was to get away from my family. That is why I accepted you. You rescued me. I will always be grateful to you for that, Avery."

He felt a strange tightness in his chest. He wanted to tell her he didn't want her gratitude, but he was not sure exactly what he did want. "I'm happy to have been in a position to help you," he said awkwardly. "I do not want you to regret marrying me."

"I don't think I regret it." She lifted her eyes to his. "Do you?"

"I don't think I regret it either."

He should move away. He knew it. Their voices had sunk too low, too intimate for so large a space. But the light, fading in a shimmer of dust motes, gave a sense of unreality that freed him. He wasn't Prescott Avery. There was no Jane, Emmet, or Katie. There had never been an Elizabeth. There was only this beautiful woman before him.

He leaned in and kissed her.

It was as though time, which had been slowed down in a still, deep pool, now broke through the dam with a white-water rush. Her response was passionate, urgent. He realized he had only meant to brush her mouth in the kind of kiss he had shared with Elizabeth. But she was somehow giving and demanding at the same time, and he found he wanted nothing more than to drag her closer and plunge them both deeper into the swirling sensuality of the moment.

There was a little shriek of dismay from the doorway. Avery jumped back from Gillian and clasped his hands behind his back in a vain and vaguely comical attempt to pretend he had not been doing anything.

It was Jane. Jane wearing Elizabeth's expression of absolute horror and revulsion. He suddenly felt physically ill.

"What are you doing?" his daughter demanded shrilly. "What are you doing hiding out here, kissing?" She spat out the word like something foul. "It's disgusting, Papa! We need you in the house.

Katie looks to be catching a cold and will most likely die of it, but you can think of nothing but kissing.'' She set her hands on her waist and glowered at him with a fierceness that would have made him laugh if he had not felt so irritated.

"Jane!" he said in a sharp tone he had not used since before Elizabeth died. "That is quite enough. One more disrespectful word to either of us, and you will spend the rest of the evening in the nursery by yourself."

Jane looked mutinous, but kept silent.

Avery turned to Gillian, but the woman he had been kissing was gone. In her place was the smilingly pleasant but resolutely distant woman he had married.

Chapter Five

"Tudding!" Katie enthusiastically dug her spoon into the bowl and slopped half its contents onto the table.

"Oh, Katie, don't do that!" Gillian tried to wipe up the sticky globs, but succeeded only in getting it on her sleeves. "You have to eat it, not play with it." Katie obligingly tried to help her clean up, but ended up knocking her bowl off the table entirely.

Gillian looked to Avery for help, but he was in the middle of a game with Emmet that involved shouting in mock terror while his son pretended to be a bear savaging his roast beef. At least this way he didn't seem to object that it was brown.

"Jane, you're not eating anything." She squatted on the floor as she tried to scoop the ruined pudding back into the cracked bowl.

"I don't like this food."

"Well, do try to eat something." She tried to

think of her mother's rules when she was a child. "Eat two bites of everything."

Katie began pounding her spoon on the table. Between Emmet's roaring and Katie's banging, Gillian was beginning to get a terrible headache. Avery, however, did not appear to notice the noise.

Why had he kissed her? It was painfully obvious that the man was still grieving over his first wife and completely absorbed in his children. Still, in the barn she had felt for the first time that he was human, perhaps even lonely. And then he had kissed her. And not just a kiss, but a kiss full of passion and promise . . . . She tried to push the memory from her mind.

"Papa does not say I have to eat two bites of everything." There was a challenging expression in Jane's gray eyes. "Papa!" she called out above the racket. "I'm not hungry. May I be excused?"

Avery looked up with a smile. "Of course, my sweet."

Jane slid off her chair with a look of sly triumph.

No. It was too much. If she did not make a stand now, it would be so much harder later. "I told her she must have two bites of everything before she is excused," Gillian said.

"That's enough roaring out of you, my young cub." Avery gave Emmet a stern look. He turned to Gillian and Jane. She could see him weighing the resentment of his already sulking daughter against gainsaying the authority of his wife. "Gillian is right," he said firmly. "Sit down and have two bites of everything. We don't want you fading away to nothing."

"Papa!"

"Sit, Janie."

Gillian shot him a look of gratitude, but he had

turned back to Emmet. Very well, a minor victory anyway.

Her triumph was cut short when she received a direct hit in the head from Katie's bread pudding catapult.

"I torry." The little girl looked more mischievous than contrite.

Emmet and Jane shrieked in triumph, and even Avery could not help the small twitches at the sides of his mouth.

She was mortified, but there was nothing to do but take it in good grace. "Very good aim, Katie!" she exclaimed. "Now I shall have something ready in case I am hungry before bedtime." She could feel a blush creeping up her cheeks, but there was no point in getting overset. She drew the little girl into her lap and tried to scrub off the bread pudding that now coated them both. "You and I are so covered in food we are a mobile picnic. Mrs. O'Connor will not have to feed us for a week."

"You have some on your forehead," Emmet volunteered.

Gillian put the wriggling Katie on the rug and wiped at her face.

"Perhaps I forgot to warn you in my letter that they were a pack of savages," Avery said with a faint smile.

It was the first sign she had seen that perhaps he had a sense of humor. Katie pulled herself up on Gillian's skirts, took a few awkward, limping steps, and then collapsed back onto all fours and crawled over to Avery.

"You've had the doctor look at her, of course." She knew he would know what she was talking about.

The humor had gone out of his face. Instead he

looked at her with an expression that was coolly repressive. "Yes."

"I think with a brace to straighten her leg as she grows . . . my friend Lydia's younger brother had one as a child, and now he walks perfectly well."

"And this makes you more of an expert than the doctor?" His eyes were cold in his inexpressive face.

She rolled her eyes and gave an uncomfortable laugh. "Of course not. I merely meant—"

"We like Katie the way she is," Emmet said loudly. "We don't want anyone to fix her."

Avery's eyes met hers. "Exactly."

They made an interesting tableau, Avery with Emmet by his side and Katie at his feet. Aware of the symbolic stance being made, Jane slid off her chair and went to stand with them.

Gillian had no choice but to swallow her annoyance. It wasn't as though she was suggesting Katie was a kind of oddity. She was only thinking that there was perhaps no need for the child to suffer. She smiled. "You look as though you are posing for the most sour-looking family portrait in history. Come and finish your dinner, Janie. I will have Mrs. O'Connor bring up the apple tart she made this afternoon."

Katie left the shelter of her father's knee and scrabbled over to Gillian. "Tart," she said clearly.

Gillian smoothed her hand over the child's white-blond curls. "At least I know how to win your affection," she said, dissecting another large clump of bread pudding from among the ringlets.

Avery gave Janie a little push toward her chair. "Finish up, my sweet." He turned to Emmet. "And tell your stepmother that we know she has very good intentions toward Katie—and that she has an enormous gob of bread pudding hanging over her left ear.''

The tension was broken, and they both laughed. "I think I will need a bath tonight." She removed the lump of food and examined it ruefully. She looked down at Katie, who was placidly wiping her runny nose with the hem of her gown "And I know that this little savage will, too. In fact, I think it would be a good idea if you all had baths."

Emmet looked injured. "I don't want a bath. I had a bath yesterday."

"It is Sunday! We don't have baths on Sunday," Jane chimed in.

"Emmet, you fell in the mud. I know Bitsy took care of the worst of it, but still you must be filthy. In another day or two, we shall have flowers growing out of your hair."

"Mama never made us have a bath on a Sunday," Janie muttered, her eyes narrowed.

The girl said it as though it was a spell, as though the mere mention of the saintly Elizabeth would send her stepmother away screaming. "Well," Gillian said briskly, sweeping up Katie as she stood, "you'll have to pretend it isn't Sunday, then, because you are all having baths. I'll have Bitsy start the water heating."

Avery looked up from his paper when she finally came downstairs. "You handled that very well," he said, standing up in a formal gesture of politeness that Gillian waved away.

"Thank you," she replied, rolling down her damp sleeves. "I'm certain you thought from the screams that Bitsy and I were murdering them, but

I assure you they are both still alive." She shot him a teasing glance. "You did have only two, correct?"

"I hope Emmet didn't bite you," he said mildly. "He's going through that bear phase, you know."

She sat down in a wing chair by the fire and rubbed her tired neck. "He snapped at Bitsy, but she was too quick for him. I think we have managed to convince him there is nothing bears like better than to go splashing about in rivers catching fish. I believe I read that somewhere. I regret mentioning the splashing part, however."

Avery was regarding her with an odd expression. "You manage them like an expert animal trainer," he said, smiling.

She leaned her head back in the chair and laughed. "You flatter me, sir. I was informed no less than six times that Mama would never have treated them so ill."

He was silent for a moment, his lips compressed. "They will use that against you often. For a time. Until they forget her."

The sadness in his voice gave her a strange pain between her ribs. "I will not let them forget Elizabeth," Gillian said quietly.

And Avery would never forget Elizabeth. The envy she felt was ridiculous. She herself didn't love him. She had merely married him to get herself out of a wretched situation. Why should she care if he still carried a torch for his first wife?

"We married very young," he volunteered unexpectedly. "Though no one was surprised. Our families had always been friends."

"A perfect match," she said, careful to keep her voice neutral.

He smiled sadly. "Yes. But her health was never good. She was an invalid for months after Emmet was born. She never should have had Katie, but she wanted another child so badly. She was horrified when she saw that Katie was deformed. She could never abide things like that. Such delicate sensibilities. She died three days later from childbed fever."

His face was tense with grief. Gilliam had the sudden urge to put her arms around his shoulders and tell him it wasn't his fault, that he couldn't have known the consequences. But she stayed where she was.

"I'm sorry," she said at last, feeling helpless. She felt self-conscious looking at him and so turned her gaze to the fire dancing around a log in the hearth.

Avery shifted in his chair. He picked up his newspaper, cleared his throat, put down the newspaper again, and got up to pour himself a drink. He took a large gulp and set the glass down with a bang. "There is something we still need to discuss."

He began pacing the room with long, restless strides. She had a feeling she knew what he was thinking. It had to do with that kiss. She wanted to tell him not to worry about it, that it meant nothing. Nothing had changed. But it had.

"What?" she asked anyway.

He took a deep breath. "I have children, as you know."

"Yes, I believe I've met them."

His dark brows crept toward each other. "Yes. Well. And Emmet is my heir."

"I'm aware of that, too."

He strode to the table, took another drink and then turned to face her. "Dash it all, Gillian. Don't make me squirm. You know well enough what I am trying to say. I do not wish for more children."

His blue eyes were blazing as though he were furious with her, as though it were her fault that they were in this ridiculous situation, this ridiculous marriage, having this utterly ridiculous conversation. "You mean you will not consummate our marriage," she said with a calm she did not feel.

His gaze fell to the hearth and then crept up to the ceiling, never meeting hers. "I married you so my children would have a mother." He strode over to his chair, sat down, and then immediately stood up again to resume pacing. "It has nothing to do with you, you understand."

"Of course." It didn't really salve the inexplicable rejection she felt. This shouldn't surprise her. In fact, it should relieve her. After all, her mother had given her to understand that her marital duties would be burdensome, if not truly unpleasant. And before today, before this afternoon, she would have been perfectly content to live out the rest of her life parting at their respective bedroom doors. But then he had kissed her.

"I wish I had known earlier of your innocence. Somehow that changes everything. I feel like I am denying you—well, that is, I never intended . . . I mean, I . . . dash it all. I wish you *had* been ruined," he said passionately, running his hand through his dark curls. "It would have made this a good deal easier."

"I'm sorry to not have obliged you." What else was there to say? "But I do not see that it makes any difference. If you remember, I did not mean to marry at all." It was true. It made no sense that she felt a strange sense of loss. Mere vanity, she told herself sternly.

"And it has nothing to do with your person." Avery picked up the small mantel clock, held it up to his ear, and then shook it. "You are an attractive woman, I'm sure. That isn't it at all." He opened the back, extracted a tin soldier, and then meditatively listened to it again. "That isn't it at all," he repeated. He drew out his watch and looked at it, then carefully reset the hands of the clock.

"You don't need to make excuses for your decision, Avery," she reminded him gently. There would be no need to find out if her mother was correct or not. But her traitorous mind took her back to the barn and the wild rush of desire she had felt in his arms. Something in his kiss had awakened a fierce part of her that insisted that she did indeed want to test the theory, and that there was every reason to believe her mother might have been wrong.

"Yes. Well." He put the clock back on the mantel and turned to face her. His eyes were startlingly pale under the darkness of his brows. "It isn't that I don't desire you, Gillian." His mouth was tight, as though the words were forced out of him. "It's just that I do not wish to desire you."

"Yes," she said quietly. "I know just what you mean."

Chapter Six

"Really Prescott, I don't know what you thought you were about, marrying that woman." Louisa ran her finger along the mantelpiece and then examined her gloved finger. "You know she'll very likely turn out like her mother—a brazen and managing creature if I ever saw one."

"Ah, yes, and so very unlike my brazen and managing sister," he said mildly, not looking up from the letter he was writing.

"Don't be horrid," she snapped. "Or I shall scratch you as I did when we were children." A smile pulled at her severe countenance. "I don't know how Mama was ever school friends with that woman. Even she admits that Lady John Harwell is sadly changed. Every time the woman opened her mouth, it was to criticize something. You must admit she is a hundred times worse than I am."

"Oh, a thousand times, surely."

"And if your new wife should end up like her?"

His pen continued to move smoothly across the paper. "I should have to pack her off to your house." He stopped and looked over what he had written. "But she will not turn out like her mother."

Louisa made a noise that in a lesser woman would have been deemed a snort. "Let us hope not." She crossed to the window and held back the heavy curtain. "Look at her, running about like a zany. You'd think she never saw snow before." She shook her head. "You thought you were getting a mother for your children. What you really got was another child."

Avery looked up from his correspondence with a sigh. "On the contrary, she is getting along much better with the children. Katie adores her, and Emmet is delighted to have someone who will play with him. You know Jane has a good deal too much dignity to do so most of the time." He did not mention that Jane still refused to speak to Gillian except when forced.

His sister turned, her hands on her hips. "Much better, you say. So it wasn't all roses at first."

"We have had our difficulties," he admitted.

"Well I'm not surprised, the poor dears. Forcing a stranger upon them. You should have let them come live with Edgecott and me. My children could have kept them company."

"We have argued this point for two years, Louisa. I am not likely to change my mind now."

She turned back to look out the window. Avery heard a feminine shriek followed by a burst of laughter.

"A good deal too much levity, in my opinion."

Louisa twitched the drapes closed in a gesture of disgust.

"I find it refreshing."

"And far too pretty. You know what people are saying, Prescott. It doesn't look proper, you going out and marrying some exotically beautiful, unknown creature—who is nothing like Elizabeth, I might add."

He turned back to his letter. "I would not wish her to be like Elizabeth."

"Prescott, really!"

He tossed her a look over his shoulder. "You know what I mean. No one could replace Elizabeth. I should not like to try." He certainly could not imagine his first wife running about in the snow with Emmet. Neither her constitution nor her nature would have allowed it.

Louisa sniffed. "At least Elizabeth took my advice. When I told Gillian I would give her my recipe for a mustard plaster, she told me she already had one that was doubtless better. Probably some wretched concoction from her mother. Everyone in the family uses my mustard plaster. Your Mrs. Ahern swears by it."

"Yes, we could have made our fortunes manufacturing it."

"Really Prescott, your joking is most inappropriate."

He smiled placidly at her. "I'm sorry. Go on. You were explaining how unbiddable my new wife is."

"She told Mother she thought Katie's lameness could be improved with a brace. And"—she drew a breath through her nose and shook her head—"she said seven is not too early to learn French. Rather than believing it is harmful to a young girl's brain, she thinks it will be easier for her to learn a language when she is younger."

"And heaven forbid we have another strong-willed woman in the family."

Whatever his sister's objections regarding mustard plasters, French lessons, and even leg braces, it was rather nice having someone other than Mrs. O'Connor make out the menus. That worthy woman saw no reason they could not continue to eat the same three dinners in continuous rotation for the rest of their lives. And it was pleasant to have someone play pianoforte in the evenings and take a turn reading aloud the book about pirates that Emmet insisted must be repeated a half dozen times each night.

"Elizabeth was everything the wife of a viscount should be."

"You bullied her, Louisa, and you know it." He thought of the many nights he had spent reassuring his first wife that she could not simultaneously expect to please his mother, her own mother, his sisters, her children, and him. Not to mention herself, of course. No, the idea that Elizabeth should have done anything simply because it entered her mind that she wanted to was virtually impossible to imagine.

"I did no such thing. I gave her advice, and she was glad for it. The new Lady Avery, however—"

Emmet burst into the room, breathless and red-faced. "Papa, I want to go sledding on the hill, and Gillian said I must ask you."

He was tempted by the boy's angelic face. "What did she say?" he forced himself to ask.

"She said I could," he replied, his eyes guilelessly wide.

He raised his eyebrows skeptically. "You look too

innocent to be telling the truth. What did she really say?''

Emmet's sigh deflated him. "She said I had to come in and have my luncheon with Janie and Katie."

"Well, I think you know my answer then."

"But! But!"

"Emmet." There was enough warning in his tone to make the boy heave another despondent sigh and leave the room with dramatically dragging steps. A moment later Avery heard him pounding up the stairs, bellowing to his sisters.

"Well, at least you've stopped spoiling them," Louisa said grudgingly. She peered into the Grecian urn by the fireplace. "And you have removed the collection of toys from in here. It was becoming quite an embarrassment, you know." She sat down with a sigh. "Honestly, Prescott, I know you made the best decision you could. But we know next to nothing about your wife, and what we have seen of her family is none too pleasing. You took a shocking risk in marrying her. She might turn out to be someone quite awful, and you are stuck with her."

She reached out and took Avery by the hand in an impulsive gesture. "Mama hinted that there might be a scandal in her background. I know it is too late, but I do wish we knew more about her. I just worry that her morals . . . and with such young children . . . ." She looked at him helplessly.

He detached himself from his sister's hand and turned from her. "I assure you, there is nothing wrong with her morals." Perhaps there was something wrong with his. After that kiss in the stables, he had thought of nothing else but bedding her. It was ridiculous. She was his wife. If there was anyone in this whole world he should be bedding, it was her. But something about the very strength of his attraction made him resist it.

"But what can she possibly know about raising children? I told you from the start you would be better off marrying the Widow Garth. Oh, I know she is not beautiful like Gillian, but she would have known well enough what to do with your wild creatures."

"I married Gillian. There is little point in discussing options that are no longer relevant."

"Avery, I hope you asked your sister to stay for luncheon."

He looked up to see his wife standing in the doorway, still wearing her coat. He felt the uncomfortable heat of shame rise up his collar. How much had she heard? Well, it wasn't as though Gillian had any illusions as to the nature of their marriage. He still felt the urge to take her hands and assure her that he was certain that he had made the right decision in marrying her.

He turned to his sister with a stiff smile. "You will stay, Louisa?"

His sister had the grace to look ashamed. "No, I cannot. In fact, I must be on my way now. Good day, Lady Avery." She bowed to his wife.

"Good day, Lady Edgecott."

"My sister," Avery said, once the front door had closed behind her, "is the biggest busybody ever born."

"She only cares about your welfare," Gillian said mildly. She untied her bonnet and walked over to the fire. "The children are having their luncheon up in the nursery with Bitsy. Shall I have you served up there as well, or would you prefer to eat in the dining room?'' She leaned over and ruffled her damp curls in front of the hearth.

"Where are you eating?"

"Oh." She stood up and looked at him in surprise. "The dining room, I suppose."

"Then I will eat there as well."

"Thank you." With a slightly quizzical expression, she took the arm he offered her.

They made their way into the dining room. Avery picked carefully through the cold collation and sat down before he attempted conversation. For the first time, he wondered what she thought about living here, away from her family and home. It certainly must not help to have a sharp-tongued sister-in-law and a husband who had spoken only the most inane civilities for upward of five weeks.

He cleared his throat. "Emmet seemed to be enjoying himself in the snow," he said cheerfully.

She finished chewing and swallowed. "Yes. We built the city of Moscow and then laid siege to it."

He felt a vague sense of envy. It might have been nice to run about in the snow, firing volleys of snowballs with them. "Ah, so we have a Bonapartist in our ranks."

She laughed and went back to her meal. There were several long moments broken only by the scrape of silver on china.

He searched around in his mind for another topic of conversation. "Louisa says you think Janie should start learning French. I am inclined to agree with you. She is very bright."

Gillian laid down her knife and fork and dabbed her fingers on her napkin. "She is. In fact, I think it is time for you to engage a governess. She bullies Bitsy mercilessly. But of course Bitsy is only sixteen herself and can't be expected to mind a young lady like Jane."

He rubbed his chin. "I can believe Jane a bully before I can believe her a young lady. I don't think she needs a governess just yet. But I will consider it," he added quickly, so she would not think he didn't value her opinion. In fact, he was slightly annoyed with himself for not thinking of the matter earlier. It was hard to imagine Jane so grown up that she needed a governess.

"I must ask Mrs. Ahern to make up another gown for Katie. She wears two little holes in all of her skirts from all her crawling about," she said, almost to herself.

He hoped she would not again bring up the subject of taking Katie to a bone specialist. The idea had rankled in his mind for weeks. Was he depriving his daughter of health? Or was he endangering it by exposing her delicate constitution to a treatment that would doubtlessly tax all her strength?

He looked at Gillian, but she was busy extracting a small model man-of-war from the recesses of her seat cushion.

"By all means. You know more about children's clothing than I do." At least, he presumed she did. In any case, she did not object, but smiled calmly and went back to salvaging the two wooden camels that had inexplicably gone down with the ship.

The silence stabbed him like sharp pins. It was always like this between them these days—so calmly pleasant it was painful. How could she look so cool? Was the agonizing stiltedness of their conversation lost on her? Or did she enjoy the sight of him squirming?

"Enough about the children. What of you?" His

rushed words sounded sudden and harsh in the empty room.

Her brows rose slightly as she turned to him. "What of me?" she echoed.

"Are you happy enough here? Is there anything you want? Can I send to England for anything that would make you more comfortable? Everyone is treating you well?"

Her laugh was warm but slightly dismissive. "Everything is fine, Avery. Why should it not be?"

"You want nothing?"

The expression of hesitancy in her eyes was gone so quickly he was not at all certain it had been there at all. "What is it?" he asked.

"I was thinking . . ." she began, with a comical expression of reluctance.

"Yes?" What could she possibly want? Perhaps she wished to visit her family or needed something to be sent to her from home. The life he offered her was excruciatingly dull, he knew. Perhaps she wished to go to more parties or the weekly assembly in Newcastle West.

She drew a breath. "I was thinking we should have a dinner party."

His look of bewilderment must have been incitement enough to continue.

"Your sister said you used to be very involved in local politics. If it is something you would like to take up again, we will need to entertain. I can't say that I know anything about how to host a political salon, but I'm certain Louisa will be happy to give me advice." The naughty twinkle in her eyes was quickly veiled by curling dark lashes. "And it is certainly respectable, if not absolutely expected, that we would entertain."

He hadn't thought of it. His political aspirations

had ended with Elizabeth's death, and he had never thought of reviving them. The idea was strangely pleasing.

"Would you enjoy it?" He would not put her through the agonies that Elizabeth had gone through. She had found politics both painfully dull and terrifyingly demanding. She was never one of a strong opinion and was even less able to defend it in the presence of the rather bullheaded, loud-voiced solicitors and parliamentarians that made up the politically inclined of the area. More often than not, she hid up in the nursery and pleaded a headache.

Gillian looked thoughtfully down at the table-cloth for a moment. "I believe I would. If you do not think my past would disgrace you."

"That is ancient history now." He smiled. "Besides the fact that you invented the worst of it, it was never more than hearsay at best anyway. No one will think anything of it."

She bit her lip to contain a mischievous smile. "Especially when I wrote my London friends with a very long and romantic account of our long-standing friendship and unexpectedly passionate reunion when I came here to convalesce from that dreadful indisposition I contracted in London."

He laughed. "Your aptitude in dissemblance assures your place in the political firmament." He stood up and patted her on the shoulder. "You are a character, Gillian. I do indeed wish we had had a long-standing friendship." Her shoulder was warm under his hand. The wool stuff of her gown slid across it like polished marble.

She looked up at him and smiled. "Thursday?"

"What?" His hand stopped. Her bright, laughing

eyes had driven all thoughts from his mind but one.

"Dinner? Thursday? Shall we plan to have Lord and Lady Needling? Sir Harvey will come of course, and I suppose there is nothing to do but invite the Foleys, though your mother says they are hopelessly encroaching."

Watching her mouth move as she talked was doing the most alarming things to his insides. "Indeed." He removed his hand abruptly and paced the room to put the length of the dining room table between them. "Fine. Fine. Do as you wish." He cleared his throat to signify that the subject was closed. "What are you doing this afternoon?"

"I promised Jane and Emmet I would watch them while they sledded on the big hill."

"Let's all go."

Her brows rose, but the corners of her mouth rose with them. "If you like." She lifted her shoulders. "I'm certain the children would enjoy your company."

"We shall wrap Katie up well and take her, too. It will be a real outing." He wasn't sure why he had come out with the idea, but the warm light in her smile made it seem like the best one he had ever had.

He shrugged off the feeling of uneasiness. They were friends. Companions. She had never objected to his awkwardly voiced decision not to consummate their marriage. There was no reason he could not enjoy her company without guilt. No reason at all.

As long as he remembered not to touch her, they could surely find a way to rub along tolerably well.

Chapter Seven

"Wellington could have moved his entire army from Portugal to France with less effort than it takes to mobilize these three children." Gillian laughed as she wound a scarf around Emmet.

"I'm ready," Jane reminded everyone.

Mrs. Ahern looked up from where she was attempting to put on Katie's mittens. "Of course you are, pet. You're a very good girl. It's the little one I'm worried about." She cast a dark glance at Gillian.

"I'm sure if she is kept warm and dry," she began. But there was little use in arguing. Mrs. Ahern was very firm in her doubt that Katie could survive out of doors.

"Rheumatic fever," she prophesied. "I knew a little girl just as delicate, and she died of rheumatic fever."

"But it will be so nice to let Katie get out in the

fresh air." She pulled Emmet's hat more firmly down onto his head and went to dig in a drawer for Katie's.

"She'd be much better off in a warm room without any killing drafts, ma'am." The housekeeper shook her head gravely. "I don't mean to be telling you how to raise these children, but I've raised five of my own. And I've known these ones since they were born."

Gillian kept her back turned and drew a deep breath. Of course the woman was right. Mrs. Ahern had known the children all their lives, while she herself had known them not yet two months. She looked down at the little woolen cap in her hands. Perhaps it was arrogant of her to presume she knew Katie's constitution.

"Are we ready to go?" Avery walked in carrying an enormous luncheon hamper.

She turned to him. "Are you certain we should bring Katie? I would hate for her to catch a chill."

"Rheumatic fever," Mrs. Ahern muttered.

Her husband's brows drew together. "Oh, but it would be so nice if we could all go." He picked up his youngest daughter. "Look at her. There are more coats and scarves about her than there is Katie herself! She has been so well lately. Surely it is all right. I would so love for her to see the snow."

"If you think it is all right, milord," the housekeeper said doubtfully.

"I will trust in the preventive power of Mrs. O'Connor's bread pudding, Louisa's mustard plaster, and your unsurpassed ability to dress Katie in more layers than an onion." He laughed and, to Gillian's surprise, squeezed Mrs. Ahern around the shoulders. "Now don't make that scowl and go threatening to leave me like you always do when you are crossed," he said cheerfully. "I don't know how we would survive without you. I should be obliged to move my household into your house so you could take care of us."

The placated housekeeper blushed at this praise and gave him a little shove. "Go on, then. But don't let her get wet. You come right back here if she gets the least bit damp."

Gillian followed the little group as they went downstairs. She felt strangely left out of their little world. She stifled the feeling. She had not been here long. Things would change. She would grow used to mothering, and it would not seem so strange. She would know how to placate and flatter Mrs. Ahern, how to ignore Lady Edgecott's comments, and how to talk to her husband.

"You know she has Katie's well-being in mind," Avery said apologetically as the small, noisy, and hopelessly disorganized cavalcade set off toward the sledding hill.

"Of course she does," Gillian replied. "And perhaps you are right to wrap her in cotton wool."

"She looks very much wrapped in cotton wool now." He looked back at where Katie rode on the sled. She looked more like a shapeless bale of cloth than a child.

"Snow, Papa! Snow!" the bundle shouted.

Gillian smiled. "I did not mean to make you go against your best judgment, Avery."

His expression was serene. "As long as we do not stay out too long, I think we will manage well enough. I have likely been too cautious of her health."

The December sun was bright, and Gillian, as her boots crunched across the snow, was unable to quell a faint feeling of optimism.

"Papa, watch me! Watch me!" Emmet launched himself headfirst down the hill on his sled.

"Mind the wall at the bottom!" Gillian called after him. Then she laughed. "I never thought I would be saying such things. I was always such a daredevil myself, it is odd to hear myself being the voice of caution."

"Daredevil?" Jane demanded.

Gillian was amused to see that the girl was curious in spite of herself. "Well, I was my parents' only child, and there were not many children on the estate where I grew up," she explained. "I was left to my own devices much of the time, and I'm afraid I was harum-scarum in the extreme." She held out her gloved hand to help Janie over the low wall at the top of the hill, but Avery's daughter stubbornly ignored her. Gillian was glad to see that Avery, who had swept up Katie and was lifting the provision-laden sled over the wall, had missed the exchange.

"The fashion at the time was not for sledding, but for ice skating," she continued, unperturbed. "I invented a game that involved swinging out over the pond on a rope tied to a tree branch and then landing full speed on my skates. As was inevitable, one day I broke through the ice."

"What happened?" Avery and Jane demanded in unison.

She laughed. "Well, I suppose if there had been any justice in the world, I would have drowned. But I managed to drag myself out and ran wailing my indignation to my mama." She cocked an eyebrow at Avery. "You have met her. You can imagine her sympathy was not what one could have wished."

"But you could have died," Jane said in a censorious tone.

Gillian bent down to unload Mrs. O'Connor's

bounty from the sled. "I suppose by that time I had cheated death so many times that she was unimpressed. I have mended my ways though." She presented the sled to Jane. "So I don't want to hear of any wild tricks on your part."

"I am very sensible," Jane informed her haughtily. In another moment she was shrieking and laughing at the top of her lungs as she whizzed down the hill.

By this time Emmet had floundered back up the hill again. "Did you see me? Did you see the birds fly up when I came toward them? Go down with me, Papa! The sled goes ever so much faster when you are on it."

It didn't take much to convince her husband to climb behind Emmet and go flying down the hill. Gillian shaded her eyes with her hand and watched them grow smaller as they sped away. The hill was made for sledding. It had a long shallow slope, a bit of a flat run, and then a second, steeper slope. Emmet's sled tipped over at the bottom of the hill, just short of the wall, and Avery scrambled to his feet and turned back to wave at her. She felt a pinch in her chest. It was almost as though they were a family. A normal family where everyone enjoyed being together. She saw Jane coming panting up the hill and blinked rapidly a few times to make certain she was suitably composed.

"I want to take Katie down."

"Oh, Janie, I'm not certain that she is old enough to go sledding."

"You can't have her come and then not let her in on the fun." Janie picked up her sister by her middle and waddled over to the sled with her. The child looked comically oversized in her arms.

Gillian glanced over to where Avery and Emmet

were engaged in shoving snow down each other's collars. "No, Katie is too big for you to hold. I will go down with her and make sure she doesn't fall off. Will you let me borrow your sled?"

Jane grudgingly allowed her to seat herself, and in another moment she and Katie were streaking down the hill so fast that their eyes streamed. They gradually slowed to a stop, and she found she was laughing loudly.

She looked down at Katie, who was pink-cheeked and squealing. "Again! Again!" She struggled out of Gillian's arms and wallowed about in a rather comical attempt to crawl up the snow-covered hill.

"Gillian, what were you thinking?"

Avery was looming over them, strikingly dark in the whiteness of the landscape. His brows were pulled tightly together. "What if she catches cold from too much exposure or, God forbid, if she had fallen off?" He swept Katie up and held her protectively to him.

Gillian took up the sled's lead and began walking up the hill beside him. "I was very careful, Avery. I wouldn't let her come to any harm, you know."

"Sled, Papa! Sled!" Katie shouted.

"If she was to sled at all, you should have let me take her." His voice was faintly reprimanding.

She fought the urge to defend herself. After all, she never claimed to know anything about children at all, much less Avery's children. They climbed the hill in silence. "I'm sorry. I shouldn't have done it without discussing it with you. But it did seem unfair to bring her if she couldn't have a go. She isn't made of china, you know," she said gently. She glanced ruefully at Katie, who was dragging on the lapels of his greatcoat and giving lusty shouts.

"I know," he sighed. "I just worry about her."

She turned to him. "You're afraid of losing her, too."

He held her gaze for a moment and then turned his attention back to Katie. "Yes."

She lay her gloved hand on his sleeve. "We won't let anything happen to her," she said confidently. She wasn't sure how, and she wasn't even certain why, but she knew she would fiercely protect Avery and his family. Katie gave a squirm and tried to launch herself from Avery's arms. Gillian's hand met his as they steadied the child.

"I know," he said, in a low voice. He turned back to where Emmet was loudly demanding the return of the second sled.

They spent the rest of the afternoon toiling up the hill in order to experience the few brief moments of bulleting flight on the way down again. Emmet invented a game in which two people raced each other down the hill. Whoever passed the big elm first got to rub snow in the face of his challenger. The loser could hope to salve his pride by attempting to go farthest before stopping and therefore earn the right to have his sled pulled up the hill for him.

Gillian spent a great deal of time with an uncomfortably cold face, dragging two sleds up the hill.

"Everyone gets one more go before we return home," Avery announced firmly. He brushed the snow off Gillian's woolen cap with an expression of fond resignation. "You look fairly frozen."

"No," she panted, stripping off her gloves to press her cold hands against her flushed cheeks. "I am having a wonderful time. Truly." She could not hope to make him understand that this camaraderie, this feeling of belonging was something she had never experienced. For the first time, she understood his decision to wed again to provide his children with this magical sense of companionship.

"Have a go with me?" he asked, indicating the sled waiting at the cusp of the hill.

"I'm not certain we'll fit."

He cut short her protests by catching her about the waist and pulling her toward the sled. Off balance, she sat down on it suddenly with an exclamation of surprise and belatedly remembered to tug her skirts over her ankles. Avery sat down behind her, a leg pressed to the outside of each of hers.

Several times she had gone on tandem rides with the children, but they were nothing like this. Avery was pressed closely against her, his arms wrapped around her waist. There must have been dozens of layers of clothing between them, but she could still feel the warmth of his body. They had not been so physically close together since the day he had kissed her in the stables. She tried to ignore the surge of desire that memory evoked.

"Perhaps it would be best if you did the steering and I braked," he said, his voice close to her ear.

"Certainly." It would be over in a moment. Then she could go back to minding the children and keeping out of his way. She found that her treacherous body had leaned back slightly against his broad chest and her cheek had wound up pressed against his jaw. She righted herself with a jerk and shoved over the crest of the hill.

She had meant to take the ride in the calm and dignified persona she had developed over the past weeks of marriage. But the world was a blur of white, and the sharp air that rushed into her mouth took away her breath and her resolutions. She realized her loud whoop of joy was accompanied by his own laughter.

"Mind the wall!" he shouted, gripping her more tightly around the waist.

They avoided it in a spray of shimmering snow. "I saw it," she chided him, looking over her shoulder at him.

"Stump!" He hauled back on the lead in her right hand. They turned sharply and the black hulk of the stump shot by, inches away. But the turn was too precipitous, and she could feel them heel over farther and farther and then, without warning, they plopped over into a bank of snow.

"I'm afraid I shall never be put up for the four-in-hand club," she giggled, staring up at the gray sky. It was ludicrous how happy she felt, considering that she was lying full length in the snow. Her scarf had been lost on the way down, and a steady trickle of dampness was making its relentless way down her neck.

"No permanent damage, I hope?" Avery sat up slowly from where he lay next to her. He was frosted like a sugarplum and his hat was gone.

"I'm afraid my pride will have to be taken away on a hurdle." She looked up at him with a face of laughing woe.

"Do I get to put snow in your face as punishment for putting an untimely end to the most splendid sled of my life?"

"It is the least of what I deserve," she said contritely.

His face loomed above hers. His dark curls, sparkling with water diamonds, tumbled over his forehead. She closed her eyes and pretended to brace herself for a faceful of snow, knowing he would not do it. She opened one eye. He was looking at her with a strange expression.

"Thank you." The words came out in a plume of vapor, but they were almost inaudible. "Thank you for the happiest day I have had in years."

A sudden pain in her chest made her draw up to her elbows, babbling inane disclaimers.

He silenced her with a kiss.

It was over before she knew he had done it. He grinned boyishly and got up to collect the sled and his hat, which had bailed out of the adventure at the wall.

Gillian lay where she was for a moment, savoring the warmth she felt right to the ends of her toes. Yes. It was indeed the happiest day she had had in years.

"Slow down, Emmet!" she heard Avery calling. There was the nearing hiss of runners on the snow. "Janie! Slow down!"

There was rising alarm in his voice. She stood up in time to see Janie and Emmet charging down the second hump in the hill. They were screaming their triumph at the tops of their lungs, going faster than they had ever managed to sled separately. She laughed at Avery's mother hen instincts, reveling in their childish joy.

And then she remembered the wall.

It lay half buried at the end of the hill, and they had both warned the children about it dozens of times. But no one had gone far enough to get near it in their games. It was only when they rode tandem that there was enough weight to carry them into its path.

"Left! Left!" she shouted, hoping Emmet, who was in the front, would for once recall which was his left.

Jane's feet were out, plowing the snow up as she tried to brake. Emmet made a jerky attempt to turn, but it was too late. She heard a strangled scream rise in her throat as the sled slammed obliquely into the wall and both children went flying.

Chapter Eight

It was like a nightmare in which one couldn't get one's legs to move quickly enough. Avery floundered toward where the children lay in two starkly black blotches against the snow. Janie sat up, blinked for a stunned moment or two, and then began crying. Emmet had not moved.

He heard Gillian panting through the snow behind him and knew she would take care of Janie. When he reached his son, he was relieved to see the boy's chest was heaving with the heavy gasps that followed having the wind brutally knocked out of him. Then he saw that the snow was stained with an ever-widening patch of red.

"Gillian!"

Emmet's face was a river of blood. The lower half of it was indistinguishable except for the long, horrible scream that began emanating from it. Avery felt nausea and panic at war within him.

"Gillian!" He pulled off his glove and tried to stanch the blood with it. Emmet's screams were becoming hysterical, and he writhed away from his father's touch.

"Go to Katie," Gillian ordered Janie.

Avery was dimly aware that his youngest daughter, alone at the top of the hill, had added her own wailing to the cacophony.

Gillian dropped to her knees beside him. She drew a sharp breath at the sight of Emmet's face. "Broken nose," she said tightly.

"He's going to bleed to death." He heard the panic in his own voice. Emmet would die like Elizabeth. He would watch the boy's life come flooding out and, as with her, there would be nothing he could do.

How much blood could a boy have in him? Already the front of his coat was so wet with it that the blood ran off in rivulets. A steady stream flowed down his armpit, where it melted the snow in wide scarlet pits that steamed malevolently at the edges.

"Avery, your scarf." The tone of Gillian's voice indicated that she had said it several times. He dragged his eyes away from Emmet and nearly choked himself in his haste to remove his scarf.

"I know, darling. It isn't nice at all. But you must let me press the top to stop the blood." Her soothing voice was drowned out by Emmet's screams. He was spitting and gurgling, choking on his own blood.

Avery's vision began to grow dark around the edges.

Gillian felt along the boy's neck and then rolled him onto his side. He looked worse, the blood streaming out faster than ever, but at least he seemed to breathe more easily. "There you go," she said, with awful cheerfulness. "It will stop in a moment. And the snow at the back of your neck will do more good than a key for a nosebleed."

"I'm bleedig!" Emmet howled.

The volume of his voice suggested that he might not be on the brink of death after all. Avery drew two deep breaths.

"So you are," he said, with a pathetic attempt at levity. "Bleeding like a soldier. And you are being very brave."

"Oh, yes," Gillian echoed. "And you probably saved Janie."

"I did?" Emmet's eyebrows, the only part of his face that wasn't covered with rapidly crusting blood, raised with interest.

"Certainly. You were in front. If you hadn't hit the wall, she might have. As it is, she was only bruised a bit." Gillian's eyes met his. She almost smiled.

"Not that you should have been sledding near the wall anyway," Avery reminded his son. The gentle hand he brushed through the boy's pale hair softened the censure in his voice.

"*You* did," Emmet protested. "I saw you nearly crash. And Janie and I were going ever so fast. Did you see us? We were going the fastest ever." His words were almost unintelligible with his blocked nose.

Avery pressed his son's hand. "We will discuss this later. I don't want this ever to happen again. Not to you or to anyone."

Gillian had experimentally released the pressure she was putting to the bridge of Emmet's nose. She looked up at him. "I think he'll be all right." Her smile made the tight cords within him relax slightly.

Together they helped Emmet sit up. He went white and collapsed back, near fainting. Avery looked at Gillian, the sick fear rising again in his throat.

"You'll be all right, Emmet. Just lie back until you feel a bit better." Gillian's voice was soothing them both. "I remember when my cousin William, who was the biggest bully that ever lived, broke his nose when he fell off the back of the sofa while he was pretending it was a horse. He must have bled about a hogshead's worth, and the way my mother carried on you'd think he'd severed his own head.

"But his own mother was just as calm as you please. 'Broke your nose again, did you, Willy?' " his wife imitated in a high, nasal voice. " 'It serves you right for being a fool. And now you will be a ridiculous-looking fool for weeks to come. And of course you *would* have to bleed all over your second best shirt.' " Gillian laughed, and Avery and Emmet joined in weakly. "He turned out to be a handsome devil. With a very fine nose. And went into the cavalry, of course."

"I'm all bloody," Emmet reminded her, obviously feeling that it was time the conversation returned to himself.

"You certainly are. It is quite shocking. Mrs. O'Connor and Mrs. Ahern will be thrown into fits. I daresay they will make you eat quite a lot of tea cakes as a reward for displaying such remarkable gore." She tucked one arm under his shoulders. Her eyes flicked to Avery, and she indicated that he should help her. "And only think of what a fright you will give your cousins."

They lifted him up, and Avery carried him up

the hill. Gillian followed behind him, chattering cheerfully.

"Your eyes will go quite black and your nose will swell up enormously. They will run screaming."

Avery repressed a feeling of revulsion. Why was Gillian discussing such things? Couldn't she see that his son needed comfort, not a reminder of his injuries?

"I can be a monster!" Emmet seemed quite taken with the happy thought.

"And you can tell them how much blood there was!" she agreed with a rather macabre enthusiasm.

He shot a glance at Emmet, but the boy, despite his rapidly swelling nose, seemed quite content.

"I can see a big puddle of it where I was lying," he said.

Avery did not turn back to look at it. He remembered well enough the sense of helpless panic he felt before he saw that Emmet's life was not endangered. He scowled and continued marching resolutely up the hill, where he could see Janie and Katie waiting anxiously. His son and wife continued the conversation across his back in rapidly exaggerating detail. He resisted the urge to chastise Gillian, but he could not help but feel she was being rather callous about the whole situation.

"What is happening?" Jane demanded, as soon as they were in shouting distance. "You stayed there ever so long. Is Emmet dying? It was not fair of you to leave us here when we didn't know anything."

The boy looked scornfully down from his position in Avery's arms. "I broke my nose," he announced proudly.

"You look disgusting."

"I'm covered in blood!" Emmet agreed in delight. He spread out his arms to give her the full, horrible effect.

It appeared his whole family was obsessed with reliving the unpleasant details of the accident. The gravity of the situation was lost on all of them. Most distressingly, Gillian. Didn't any of them understand Emmet could have been killed?

"Look at Katie," he snapped. "She must be near to freezing. I won't have her catching her death just because you want to stand here discussing pints of blood and blackened eyes. Janie, you take the other sled, and I will take this one. Gillian, I will trouble you to carry my daughter."

The mood stilled as though a branchful of snow had buried them in a cold deluge. Jane and Gillian obeyed him without a word, and they all started off toward the house. Emmet began whimpering again. Avery held him closer, but did not know what to say to comfort him. They continued on in painful silence.

"Papa." Janie peered around the edge of the door. Her gray eyes were big in her anxious face.

"Come in here, my dear. What is bothering you?" He pushed away the ledger he had been staring at for the last half hour and patted his knee. His daughter padded over and seated herself gravely on his lap.

"I want you to tell me the truth, Papa," she said in a stern, grown-up voice.

"I will," he promised.

"What did the doctor say?"

He smiled and smoothed his hand down her long, fair braid. "He said Emmet has a broken nose."

Jane looked down at her hands. "Will he die?" she asked at last.

He covered her small hands with his own. "No. Most decidedly not."

"Are you certain?"

He smiled, relieved that he was indeed certain. "Yes."

The girl's face relaxed somewhat. "And Katie?" she prodded.

"What about Katie?"

"Has she caught her death?"

Knowing that she would be insulted, he refrained from laughing. "No, my dearest. Katie hasn't caught her death. I think she is tougher than we give her credit for. I'm sorry I worried you when I predicted she would." He looked her in the eyes. "I was upset because I was worried about Emmet. I shouldn't have been so cross."

She gave a worldly little sigh. "I thought as much."

Avery wished life had not made her so serious so quickly. She should be laughing and playing, not worrying if her brother or sister were going to be taken from her as cruelly and capriciously as her mother was.

"I don't understand my stepmother," Janie said suddenly.

He looked up from where his gaze had come to rest on the fire in the grate. "Why is that?" he asked, though he wasn't certain if he understood Gillian either.

"Instead of being kind to Emmet and coddling him and giving him all manner of sweets, like Mrs. O'Connor and Mrs. Ahern do, she tells him how dreadful he looks and tells him awful stories about her cousins' broken arms and cut heads." She shook her head. "I cannot like it."

There was something in her tone and gesture that reminded him so forcibly of Louisa that he struggled not to laugh.

"I suspect she is only trying to distract him from his woes. With Mrs. O'Connor and Mrs. Ahern, he hardly needs someone else to coddle him, now does he?"

A frown formed between her pale brows, and her small mouth pinched. "I think she is unfeeling."

He tried to push the frown away with his thumb. "I don't think so," he said gently. "Emmet seems to like hearing about how awful he will look, so it is her way of cheering him up. I can't say I would like that method it if were my nose that were broken, but for him it works very well."

He hadn't thought so at the time, his conscience prodded. He had snapped at her and condemned her as thoughtless when it was she who had been so marvelously calm about the accident. When both Emmet and he himself were panic-stricken, she had soothed them and competently stopped Emmet's bleeding. No one could have handled the situation better. Not himself, not Louisa, not even Elizabeth.

"A proper mother would be kind to him," Jane said darkly.

"She is kind. I think she cares about you all a good deal." He had not thought about the words before he said them, but now he realized they were true. She had done so much to show that she did care for them, even though she had never laid eyes on them until recently. Why? They were certainly not reciprocative. For his sake? The thought gave him a peculiar tightness in his chest.

Jane slid off his lap and stood in front of him

with her arms crossed. "I liked things better without her, Papa. She is a bad influence on Emmet, and I don't like to think of Katie growing up like her."

He leaned over and pinched her cheek. "You have been listening to your aunt, haven't you? Give her a chance, Janie. You're a fair girl; give her a fair chance." He smiled faintly. "She is a change, and everyone dislikes change, but I think she might end up being a good change. For all of us."

Chapter Nine

"It is a shameful thing that the Irish parliament should have been disbanded," Sir Harvey said for the fourth time. He had made significant progress through a bottle of sack after dinner, and the effects were becoming rather obvious. "Shameful, I say! The idea that we should have to be put to the expense of going to Westminster for half the year to make our voices heard to a bunch of small-minded prigs who haven't a donkey's notion of how policy should be made here . . ."

Avery saw, to his horror, that Sir Harvey's thick forefinger was outstretched toward his wife.

"You," he jabbed again. "You're one of them. One of them London types. What have you to say about it?"

"Really, Sir Harvey," Lady Needling tittered. "Though Lady Avery is recently from London, she cannot have any awareness of the political situation

there. We poor females must fill our minds with less
lofty things." She look the cup of tea her husband
proffered. "My goodness, but you sat long after
dinner, Charles. I hope you are not drunk. You
smell like a distillery." She ignored his scowl and
turned a pleasant smile on Gillian. "Lady Avery,
you are much more likely to be versed in the newest
fashion for bonnets than the feelings of those
dreadful, prosy parliamentarians."

"Indeed, is it high crowns this year?" Mrs. Foley
asked eagerly.

"High crowns with enormous pokes," Gillian
replied. She turned to Sir Harvey. "I sympathize
with your situation, sir, but the Irish Parliament
was dissolved back in '01. Whether you approve of
the Act of Union or not, we will have to live with
it. I think the question more to the point is what
do you propose to do about the situation *now*?"

Dear God, what was she going to do? Get in a
political discussion with the idiot? The man was
half drunk and had already worked himself into a
state of dudgeon. It would never do to get into a
row with him. Why couldn't they simply have tea,
light conversation, and perhaps some pianoforte
after dinner as they were supposed to do?

"Revolution, Bertram?" Lord Needling asked
caustically.

"The Americans did it," he fired back.

"The Americans had a great deal more sea
between them and the motherland than we do at
present," the tall, austere man replied.

Gillian looked up at him with an appreciative
nod. "Furthermore, any Irish political independence would require the support of the people.
Once they attained their freedom, they would not

be at all likely to wish for us, a religiously separate, elite, land-owning class, to remain in control."

He stared at his wife in surprise. It was a remarkably perceptive thing to have said. He felt a tiny ember of pride glow brightly inside him.

"It'd be the guillotine for you, Harvey. Just like with them Frenchie nobs." Mr. Foley laughed loudly. "Citizen O'Reilly would hardly be anxious to keep you provided with your hunters and your fine house."

"I think Lady Avery has made a good point," Needling said, ignoring him.

Avery smiled. He and Gillian had occasionally spoken of politics during their evenings alone, but it was surprising to hear her voice her opinions so articulately. Perhaps it was not quite the thing to have a wife who could acquit herself so well in an arena so generally dominated by men, but he found it a novel pleasure.

He cast a sympathetic glance to where Lady Needling's sister, a hopelessly dull creature invited to make the numbers even, was playing quietly on the pianoforte. While Gillian continued her lively argument with the men of the group, the women drifted over to the instrument. Miss Graystone continued to play while the other women stood about her making enthusiastic, inane comments on her skill.

Their husbands continued in their animated discussion with his wife. Perhaps it was rude of his guests to have continued the political conversation after dinner, but that could not be helped. If Elizabeth had been here, she might have made certain the conversation was guided along cheerful, neutral lines. Actually, she would probably have been with the other women, who had moved on to making enthusiastic, inane comments about the color of the wall hangings.

"What do you propose to do, Miss Gad-about-London?" Harvey roared.

Avery scowled at the man. He would call the man out in a heartbeat if he dared to insult Gillian.

"It's Lady Gad-about-London, if you please," she corrected him, her smile mischievous. She put her finger to her lips and thought for a moment. "I think my course of action would be rather unexciting, I'm afraid. I'm not as well-versed in the situation as all of you gentlemen, of course, but it seems to me the best thing to do would be to concede what we must at the moment, and direct our efforts toward the Regent. He's Whiggish now, mainly to plague his father, and with men of influence around him, he may be inclined to look on our situation more favorably. But I think he may change his tune when he becomes king. His father cannot last much longer, I think."

Foley was looking at her as though she were an exotic creature from the tower zoo. Needling swept her an elegant bow. For some reason, his look of admiration rankled Avery. It was better than him laughing at her, to be certain, but he didn't have to look so damned besotted.

Sir Harvey himself looked stymied for a moment, then burst into a loud laugh. He turned to Avery. "Where did you find this creature, Avery? She has windmills in her head, but at least she has *something* in there." He clapped Gillian on the shoulder with such vigor that Avery worried for her safety. "Here we were, set to mill each other down, and I'd clean forgot you were a woman. Oh, but it is nice to meet a lady who can talk about more than children or fashion or their infernal aches and pains."

She laughed. "I assure you, I am not the least bit extraordinary. I merely listen to what my husband says." She shot him a look of pleased triumph. "All my political knowledge comes from his very patient explanation. Now, the ladies must be bored to flinders. Enough of this talk. There is time to change the world tomorrow. Tonight, it is my duty as hostess to see you are well entertained."

She stood up and gracefully excused herself to go to the ladies, who appeared to have run out of conversation and lapsed into an enthusiastic and inane silence.

"She's a right'un, Avery," Foley said approvingly. "And it's just like you to land in a pot of jam. We'd never even laid eyes on her before you were leg-shackled."

He tried not to look too smug. It was very pleasant to find that his friends found his wife admirable. Louisa would be irked to no end.

"She is, indeed, remarkable," Needling agreed. "I can't think of when I've spent a more pleasant evening. I'm glad you're entertaining again, Avery. We've missed you sorely. You'll be going to London for the spring session, I gather?"

Foley leaned back in his chair and laughed. "And seeing that Lady Avery is from London, she won't kick up dust about it, like my wife does. Always dead set on going. Thinks she'll be the kick of fashion, and in two weeks she has the megrims and wants to go home."

"I'm not certain what our plans are." Thinking about the future with Gillian seemed strange. In the deep recesses of his mind, he had somehow always thought of this as a temporary arrangement. It occurred to him now that he would likely be married to Gillian infinitely longer than he had been married to Elizabeth. He shifted in his chair and pushed the thought away.

Lady Needling began singing, accompanied by her sister on the pianoforte. Avery could hear Gillian patiently satisfying Mrs. Foley's minute interrogation regarding the bonnet question. It occurred to him with a jolt that he easily could have married a witless ninny who would have left him bored senseless after a few minutes nattering about the latest gossip, or a shrewish creature who would badger the patience out of him.

"Yes, I suspect we will go to London for the session," Avery said thoughtfully. It was high time he did, of course. He'd been out of mourning over a year.

"Afraid your wife will outshine you?" Sir Harvey guffawed.

"I have no doubt of it," he replied, grinning. "She is eminently my superior in every way."

"Likely so, you lucky dog."

He merely smiled.

The rest of the evening was pleasantly dull. Gillian made certain everyone enjoyed themselves, and when Harvey showed an interest in reviving their former conversation, she deftly turned it in other directions.

At last they waved good-bye to the last coach as it rolled down the drive into the rain.

Gillian sighed and looked up at the dark sky. "Lady Needling said it was drizzling, but I would have to say that this is much more like a mizzle. Much finer raindrops than an ordinary drizzle." She grinned at him. "Am I correct? I think I am getting much better. After dozens and dozens of morning calls, I think I am becoming quite an expert in discussing the Irish rain."

"Definitely mizzling," he replied with a wry smile. "I don't know what Lady Needling was thinking. But, of course, she is from Cork, and therefore must be excused her ignorance of Limerick rain." He followed his wife back into the house, annoyed with himself for having been so ill-tempered all evening.

"Dear God, I thought they'd never leave." Gillian flung herself into a drawing room chair and threw a dramatic hand over her forehead.

"You seemed to be enjoying yourself," he said.

She sat up. "Oh, Avery, you're not cross with me, are you? It was dreadful of me to spend the evening arguing politics." She took off her slippers and stretched out her stockinged feet to wiggle her toes. "I know I came across as monstrously forward, opinionated, and shockingly blue, but I really couldn't help myself."

He went to the fire and began to bank it for the night. He suddenly felt strangely shy. "On the contrary, I think you acquitted yourself very well," he said, not looking at her.

"You did not find me too dreadfully forward?" She smiled.

"I enjoyed it immensely," he said. "You are always a pleasant surprise to me."

She considered this for a moment. "That is most likely the kindest thing you have ever said to me."

It was more than the fire that made his face feel warm. Had he really never said anything more romantic? "Well, it's true," he said lamely.

He turned to her and leaned on the mantelpiece. "I wish I could express myself as well. I am afraid I am far too conciliatory to be a good member of parliament."

She looked up at him, her brown eyes bright.

"Oh, that is not true, Avery. You are a born moderator. You dislike conflict and extremes. When Foley and Harvey nearly came to blows over whether the woodcock was cooked with tarragon or with sage, you stepped in and settled it. You can't stand to hear Jane and Emmet bicker." She smiled in a way that made his stomach do a peculiar dance. "Needling said several times how much he had missed your ability to see both sides of an issue and negotiate a solution acceptable to all parties."

"Hopelessly wishy-washy," he said, smiling ruefully.

She threw a sofa cushion at him. "How dare you speak so of my husband!"

He caught the cushion and would have thrown it back at her, but her expression had changed to one of thoughtful contemplation.

"You must find me a great change," she said quietly.

He walked over and pushed the cushion behind her head. "Why do you say that?" He smoothed his hand over her curls and allowed himself to revel in the pleasant tingles that shot up his arms.

"Sometimes when you don't think I am looking at you, you have an expression on your face that seems bewildered. As though you don't know what to make of me. I know you are comparing me to Elizabeth."

The name was like a blast of cold air. He turned and walked back to the fireplace. "Of course not," he lied.

She stood up and went to him. In her stocking feet she seemed smaller, almost vulnerable. He felt an alarmingly strong urge to take her in his arms. He had always likened her to an Amazon, but now he saw a defeated sadness behind her smile. "I will never be like you and Elizabeth. I try to be conciliatory and pleasing, but I'm hopelessly hurly-burly. I tried to be a gracious hostess, I really did. It's just when Sir Harvey—''

He ran his fingers over the irrepressible tendrils that had escaped the carefully modish hairstyle her maid had labored over. "You jump in and fight battles, Gillian. I admire that. You know what you think and you say so.''

A corner of her mouth lifted in a wry smile. "You knew I was a hoyden when you married me.''

"A hoyden, an actress, and a completely un-principled teller of falsehoods,'' he agreed more cheerfully than he felt. He felt the familiar desire to kiss her and forced himself to turn away. "And a fierce reorganizer,'' he continued, with mock annoyance. "There isn't a cupboard in the house you haven't turned completely inside out and put back together in the most illogical manner conceivable.''

She trailed after him, her hands on her hips. "Merely because I arranged the books in the library by subject rather than by author—''

He turned on her. "And all my records by subject rather than by year?''

She caught her lip between her teeth and looked contrite. "Yes, that didn't really work out, did it?''

"Not after Emmet dropped the last thirty years' worth of rent records all over the study floor. I'm still trying to sort it all out.'' Despite his bantering tone, her eyes took on a look of concern. "Now, Gillian,'' he said quickly. "You know I'm only plaguing you.''

"I know. It isn't that.'' She began gathering up the teacups and putting them on a tray. "It just makes me realize how different you and I are.''

"Come now, let Mrs. O'Connor take care of that." He pulled her away from the tea tray. "It is far too late at night to be tidying. It is time for bed." He thought of her spending yet another night alone in Elizabeth's bedchamber, perhaps the only married virgin in the whole country. "We are different," he agreed. "But perhaps it isn't a bad thing."

"It was tonight," she countered. "I think I embarrassed you."

"On the contrary. I was very proud of you. No other man in the room had a wife so clever." He looked down and saw that he still held her hand. He let it go and drew a deep breath. "Elizabeth and I were perhaps too much alike," he said slowly. "We were overindulgent with the children because we hated quarreling with them. We never would have risen to the political elite because Elizabeth could not bear to hear voices raised in debate, and I, thinking myself fair-minded, but likely only shilly-shallying, could see both sides of every issue. While very placid and pleasant people, I'm sure, I wouldn't go as far as to say that we were terribly amusing."

"You're much less dull than you used to be," she said with a teasing smile. "You are marvelous with the children. In fact, I heard Louisa say you have shown a great deal too much levity of late."

He laughed. "Did she? High praise indeed."

He took up a branch of candles, and they slowly walked together up the stairs. Gillian sighed. "And I'm glad you don't mind so very much that I am not like you or Elizabeth," she said, returning to the subject they had both been silently contemplating. They came to the top of the stairs and paused.

She raised her eyes to his. "But I can't help but wish I was a little bit more like her."

For months he had wished the same thing. He had told himself that if she were just a little bit more serene, more ladylike, more Elizabeth-like, the painful ache of loss in his life would be eased. "I like you very well the way you are, Gillian," he said quietly.

She said nothing. He wondered if perhaps she did not believe him. But he was suddenly aware it was true. It made no sense at all, but it was true. They walked in silence to her bedroom door. She paused with her hand upon it. In the dimness, her eyes were dark and unreadable. The hunger he felt for her was almost unbearable. He reached out for her, aching to feel her in his arms.

His gesture was lost in the darkness. "Good night, Avery," she said quietly, turning the doorknob. "I'll see you in the morning."

Chapter Ten

Gillian hauled the Christmas pudding out of the boiling water with the handle of a wooden spoon and staggered over to the worktable. It made a rather disheartening splat when she set it down. Was it not boiled enough? Surely not. But it had been in there for ages. Her mother had always been in charge of the Christmas pudding at home, and though the woman never set foot in the kitchen at any other time of year, to her credit, the pudding was always perfect.

Rivulets of steaming water were running off the sodden mass, across the table and onto the floor. She jumped back from the splatters and gingerly gave the lump a nudge.

"Damn."

Lady John Harwell's Christmas puddings were always smooth, dense, and as perfectly spherical as a twelve-pound cannon shot. Their sultana-dotted surface gave off the soothing aroma of ginger and nutmeg. Her Papa always said it was a shame to cut into them.

With this pudding, however, it might be considered more of a mercy killing. The cloth fell away to reveal a pale, corpulent lump with a rash of sultanas on one side of its face. As she watched it, it began to . . . slouch.

"Oh dear. Not good."

"Are you having trouble, Lady Avery?" Mrs. O'Connor asked brightly. She looked up from where she was adding sculpted apple accessories to the most ravishing ham Gillian had ever seen.

She moved quickly in front of her creation. "No, no trouble! This is an old family recipe, you know. It is a bit unusual for a Christmas pudding, but my family always had it." Perhaps some foliage camouflage would improve its appearance. She turned and quickly began stabbing sprigs of holly over its pocked surface.

"Good, for you haven't got time to do another. Dinner will be served as soon as you get yourself changed. What a pity you had to throw the first two out. I hate to see food wasted."

"Yes," she said, sighing, "and even the dogs didn't seem too keen on that second one." The decidedly flat-bottomed pudding was now positively bristling with holly. She bit her lip and grimaced. It didn't look *quite* appetizing, but it would have to do.

She went upstairs to change her gown and then joined Avery and the children in the drawing room. They must have been waiting for a few minutes, because Emmet had already managed to soil both knees of his new suit with chimney soot and reduce Katie to tears.

"Now, since you are going to dine with Gillian and me on this special occasion, I expect you to act like adults," Avery said in a stern voice, as he tried in vain to brush the grime off his son. "Katie, of course, doesn't know any better, but I expect you two to mind your manners. Otherwise, next year you will have to eat your Christmas dinner in the nursery like your cousins all do."

"Can I take my new ship with me?" His son held out the model Spanish galleon he had received as a Christmas gift.

"I don't think so, Emmet. You wouldn't be able to mind it and eat at the same time."

Emmet turned to his sister. "See? Then you can't take in your new doll."

"But dolls aren't like ships! They're like people!" Janie protested.

Gillian remembered her own similar objections when she was the same age. "Dolls eat doll food," she said in a placating tone. "Your dolls can have their own Christmas dinner while we are eating ours."

Janie took this logical argument with very bad grace. With a look that suggested she was being extremely ill-used, she explained very gently to her doll that Stepmother would not allow her to attend the dinner party.

Gillian resisted the urge to throw up her hands. Nothing she did seemed to please the child.

Jane, of course, was patiently hostile. Emmet seemed to like her, but he had been a fretful invalid while he was recovering from his accident. Avery . . . well, Avery had been very appreciative of her role in nursing Emmet, and had never mentioned the dinner party again. Indeed, he had spent every evening since in pleasant, mild conversation with her. She had never again felt that strange pull, that palpable desire between them as she had that night.

Only Katie was receptive to her affection. The little girl lit up like sunshine when she came into the room. It was hard not to turn all her attention to her when she was the only one of the insular little family who ever seemed truly glad she was there.

With a feeling of foreboding, Gillian sat down to dinner. To her, Christmas always had a kind of forced joviality to it. Every year it was the same. Early inroads into the brandy would lead to vociferous arguments between relatives, followed by a silent, baleful dinner. The inevitable boiled ham and perfect Christmas pudding elicited the same high-pitched compliments, followed by a vigorous resurrection of grievances after dinner whilst one's cousins mauled the new toys. Depressed with food and the knowledge that it was only a year before it must be done again, one retired, gratefully, to bed.

She smiled tensely around the table, well aware Emmet was kicking Jane under the cloth. Katie, who sat on her father's lap during dinner, was the best behaved of the lot. She placidly contented herself with decorating the tablecloth with handfuls of potato puree and banging her spoon on the table. Avery growled at the other children, Janie sulked, and Emmet managed to dump the contents of the gravy boat down his trousers.

"Christmas is a special time," Avery said, with a wry laugh, removing Katie's greasy hands from his cravat. "I remember so many happy Christmases with my family. We always had Christmas dinner with my parents and my brothers and sisters, and then the next day, St. Stephen's Day, we would all get together at my grandmother's house and have a grand party.''

He removed Janie's glass from where it had been in immediate danger of being knocked over by her elbow as she sawed her meat.

"All the aunts and uncles and cousins would come, and there would be eating and drinking and dancing and games.'' He smiled at the memory. "The wrenboys would come to all the houses in the village, even ours, playing music. We would give them drinks and a few coins, and then they were off to the next house. A bit like caroling, I suppose. I don't suppose you had wrenboys in London.''

"I've never heard of wrenboys.'' She removed Emmet's fork from his hand, gave him a look that suggested forcibly that it was better not, while at the table, to play a game that involved stabbing one's sister, and then turned her attention back to her husband.

It was probably only a Christmas-induced homesickness that was making her feel so maudlin. She forced a brighter smile.

"I don't know where the custom comes from, going out on the wren, as it is called,'' he said. "They are called strawboys in Wexford and mummers in Kerry. I cannot find anyone who knows the least bit about the tradition, or why it is particular to St. Stephen's Day. But it has always been done, and there is no reason it should not continue.''

"Mama liked the wrenboys,'' Janie said quietly. "She used to sing a little song about it.''

Avery's eyes were soft. "Yes, I remember one

Christmas, when you were small, Janie, and Emmet was but a babe in arms. The wrenboys came to the door and the whole household came out to see them. It was at Louisa's house, and we were all there. You, Janie, went out to them and started dancing to the music, as happy as could be. Then all the children joined in. They were all dancing madly about on the lawn in the middle of the night. I will always remember it.''

"I remember that night." Janie laughed.

Gillian excused herself, muttering something about the Christmas pudding.

Of course there were a dozen servants in the house perfectly able to serve pudding, but she had to get away. Down the hall she could hear Janie laughing uproariously in a way she had never heard before.

An unexpected sob erupted within her, and she stifled it. There was no point in feeling sorry for herself. Chastising herself for her bout of self-pity, she measured out a quartern of brandy and began to heat it in a ladle. Surely she would grow used to the fact that her husband's virile good looks contained a mild soul unencumbered by passions of the animal nature.

The pudding was depressing her. She frowned at it where it lay, flaccid, on the platter, a chasm forming between the side with sultanas and the side without. "Thank heaven one is *supposed* to set it on fire," she muttered. "Or I should be obliged to start a new tradition." She held up the brandy bottle in a mocking toast, took a sip, and lit a twisted spill of paper. Trying to remember how her mother had always done it, she touched the spill to the stream of hot brandy as it poured out of the ladle.

The entire holly-covered mass went up in a heat-less explosion of blue. Gillian gave a little yelp of surprise and then stood back, rather pleased with the effect. She belatedly remembered it was a rather long way from the kitchen to the dining room and it might have been better to have lit the thing just before making her triumphant entrance. She scuttled down the hall with the tray, going as fast as she could without blowing out the flames.

"Here's the pudding!" she announced, bound-ing in the door. Her initial relief in seeing that the flames had not burnt out was quenched when she realized the holly had caught fire. Thin wisps of black smoke drifted up from the crackling foliage.

"Lovely my dear, lovely." Avery jumped to his feet and took the platter from her. He turned to the sideboard and deftly plucked out the charred remains. "No, Williams, I don't believe we will need your services. I think we will manage dessert *en famille.*" His serene smile gave no indication that he noticed the rather alarmed glances of the footmen.

"It broke in half," Emmet announced.

"What is that awful smell?" Janie pinched her nose. "Christmas pudding isn't supposed to smell like that."

Avery inhaled deeply. "It's the roasted holly. Mmmm. I haven't smelled that since I was a boy."

"It kind of stinks," his son objected.

"Oh no. It smells just as it should." He grinned at Gillian, who was unsure at the moment whether she wanted to hit him or kiss him for being so kind. "See, this is very special Christmas pudding. It is called 'Before and After' pudding." He put the platter in the place of honor in the middle of the table.

The trial by fire had not improved its appearance. Though Avery had removed the burnt holly, small bits of ash decorated the pale surface, which had now broken in two at the equator. The interior looked decidedly mushy.

"See," Avery was pointing out the break to the children. "This side represents the old year, and the side with the plums represents the new. Our new year is very full of lovely treats in store for us."

Jane looked skeptical. "I see last year wasn't very nice at all."

Avery did not appear to have heard her. "As we are very nearly between years I will slice everyone a piece with a little of the old year and a little of the new." He carefully selected the least damaged region and began sectioning. After a moment, he looked up. "Gillian, do sit down. I'll take care of it from here."

She obeyed him woodenly. It was absolutely humiliating. She should have written to her mother to make certain of the recipe. She should have practiced it. Instead she had hoped for the best and ended up with disaster. Just like everything else.

She swallowed the lump in her throat and looked down at the serving of pudding Avery had placed before her. The two sections, the before and after, as Avery had called them, leaned tiredly against each other.

"Now, since we have our Before and After Christmas pudding, it is traditional we should each say what we plan to accomplish in the coming year." Avery put a piece of pudding into Katie's grasping hands.

"Tudding!"

"Pudding," he agreed.

"Tudding," she said again through a thick mouthful.

"I plan to be a good mother to Miss Caroline, Little Lottie, and Princess Deirdre," Janie said pompously. "And I will not neglect Poor Anabelle, even though her nose is cracked and she is ugly."

"I will be a pirate!" Emmet shouted.

"That isn't an accomplishment," Jane gave him a severe look. "Being a good mother to your dolls counts as one, because someday when I am grown I will be a good mother to my own children."

Emmet rolled his eyes and thought for a few moments. "If I don't eat the pudding, do I have to say anything about next year?" He poked it with his fork. "It doesn't look like something people are supposed to eat."

"Tudding." Katie pulled a sultana out of her mouth and wiped it down the front of her frock.

In another moment Gillian was going to burst out crying. Avery would pity her and the children would think her insane. What kind of a fool cried over a silly pudding? But it wasn't just the pudding, it was everything. Before and After, Avery had dubbed it. Before her marriage, and after. And for her, the After was nothing but a vast desert of plain, blank, undercooked pudding.

Avery swallowed the last bite without chewing, his eyes watering slightly. "My resolution is that I would like to get back into politics," he said. "I have stepped out of that life for too long, and it is time for me to take my place in the house. We will go to London in the spring for the session. Then you will all have a chance to see Gillian's family. What do you think of that?"

"Lovely," she choked out, watching the children warily mush their forks into the pudding.

"Bleh." Katie pulled a piece of it out of her mouth and flung it onto the table.

"So, Gillian," Avery said in a strained voice. "What is your resolution for the new year?"

"I resolve," she said as she rose to her feet, "to never, *ever* make a pudding again."

Chapter Eleven

He knew somehow that he would find her in the stables. After her dire pudding pronouncement, Gillian had given a shaky laugh and sat down for the rest of the meal, but she had disappeared soon afterward. There was no doubt he was in for a scene.

When Elizabeth was upset, she had dissolved into floods of tears that took hours of cajoling and a vigorous application of hartshorn to stop. It seemed disrespectful to admit, even in the privacy of one's own head, that it was a side of his first wife's character he had found somewhat frustrating. He realized he had never seen Gillian in a state of high emotion.

Dreading the inevitable, he had put off looking for his wife as long as he could. However, once Bitsy had escorted the children back up to the nursery, any more procrastination would look callous.

He strode across the flagged court toward the stables. Behind him he could hear the sound of Christmas reveling in the kitchens. He felt a momentary envy of his employees, who were enjoying a happy, tearless, pudding-free night of merriment. Perhaps he could go and sit with them for a while, enjoying the music and games while his wife finished up her fit of the megrims . . . . He forced himself onward.

The stables were dark, but inside he could hear the quiet shifting of the horses as they dozed beneath their fitted blankets. The stableboys and grooms would, of course, be in the kitchens, feasting with the rest of the servants. He was glad. There was no reason the whole world had to know he and Gillian were on the outs.

He pushed open the door of the hayroom and saw the glow of a lamp hung on the back wall. It made a little halo of light around her where she sat with her back to him on a pile of oat-filled sacks. "Was there no room at the inn?" he asked with a slightly forced laugh.

She turned and looked over her shoulder at him. "No, I have come in the role of Magi to admire the fine litter of kittens born here last week." To his relief, she smiled. It did not look as though she had been crying at all. Her mouth quirked wryly to the side. "And I have furthermore exiled myself from the house until I can be trusted to speak of pudding without falling into strong hysterics."

He approached her cautiously, expecting said explosion of emotion at any moment. "Why are you hiding out here? Surely your room is more comfortable."

Her shrug was limp. "I like it here."

A strange, boyhood habit made him set the swing going as he walked past. He wondered if she was thinking of what had happened the last time they were alone in the hayroom. The memory tingled through him, dangerously sweet.

"You like sitting out here alone in the middle of the night?" he countered, forcing those thoughts from his mind.

She turned her attention back to the kittens at her feet. "I just wanted to be alone for a little while," she said, not really answering his question. "Do you need anything?"

Her tone of dismissal was obvious, but he refused to take the hint. He sat down on the pile of sacks next to her. At her feet, in a little nest of fragrant hay, lay a green-eyed tabby cat placidly nursing her four mewling offspring. "No, everything is fine," he replied. "I was just concerned."

Gillian said nothing, so they sat in silence and watched the shaky, blind kittens as they staggered about in the hay. He stole a glance at her. She looked slightly pale, tired perhaps, but certainly not hysterical. What the devil was he supposed to do? He didn't remember Elizabeth ever saying she wanted to be alone. The most logical thing to do was to grant Gillian's wish, but he was strangely unwilling to leave her.

Perhaps it was not so odd to come here late at night. It was cold, certainly, but there was something comfortable about the light of the lantern and the sounds of the animals in the next room. The smell of the stores around him evoked memories of his childhood. Strange that the haven of his boyhood had now become hers as well.

"That kitten has six toes," she said in a thoughtful tone. "Have you ever seen that before? A cat with extra toes?"

He leaned over and picked up the creature. "So it does." It protested vociferously as he examined it and then handed it over to Gillian. The kitten's rather frantic wiggling forced him to cup his hands around hers. They looked strangely small within his own. He had never thought of her as delicate before.

"I'm afraid these barn cats are so prolific that there is a high likelihood one would occasionally come out with extra bits and pieces." He leaned over her hands and stroked the kitten's velvety little nose. Its cries were growing more desperate, so she returned it to its mother to nurse with its littermates. He felt awkward, as though he now had nothing to do with his hands.

"I'm sorry about the pudding," she said at last, with a comically rueful expression.

He stifled the urge to wrap her in a fierce hug. "I never cared for the stuff anyway. The best part was always setting it on fire, and you did that quite dramatically." He had meant the comment teasingly, but her sad little sigh cut to his heart. He took her hand in both of his own. "It was just a pudding, Gillian."

"It isn't that—"

There was a tremor in her voice he knew preluded tears. Oh, please, don't let her cry. What was he supposed to do if she did? Pat her on the shoulder? Take her in his arms?

He released her fingers, knowing that in another moment he would have started stroking them. "Oh, I know the children were terrors." His hands were cold without hers, and so he shoved them into his folded arms. "They were merely overly excited. I never should have agreed to let them have Christmas dinner with us, but it seemed like a special occasion. It is a family tradition from my own upbringing. Janie is quite ladylike, but Katie is far too young, and of course Emmet shouldn't be allowed near liquids of any sort until he goes off to university."

"It was very nice," she interrupted his babblings. "It was just as Christmases should be." She made a face. "Except for the gravy boat. And the pudding, of course."

"Then what is wrong?"

She bent over to nudge a confused kitten back in the direction of its mother. Her voice was so soft that he had to lean over to hear her. "I suppose I'm just a little lonely."

"Lonely?" The thought had never occurred to him. "Well, that's only because you went and hid out here on your own in this cold, drafty, dark place. Not a good remedy for lonely, you know."

She gave him a wan smile. "It isn't that."

He tried to remember if he had ever been lonely. Never growing up, of course. As one of seven children, he was likely to suffer from not enough solitude rather than too much.

There had been dark, horrible days after Elizabeth died. Perhaps the wrenching emptiness could have been termed loneliness. But what reason on earth did Gillian have to feel that way? "Do you miss your parents?" he hazarded. Perhaps he had been thoughtless not to encourage her mother to stay longer after the wedding. After all, she was a long way away from the life and the people she had always known.

Gillian's golden-brown eyes widened slightly in surprise. "Oh, no, I don't miss them at all. If I was desperate enough to engineer my own ruination to get away from them, one could hardly think I would suddenly long to go back to them."

"Perhaps you regret your rashness," he suggested.

"I don't," she said firmly. "I suppose that is terribly wicked of me, but it is a vast relief to get away from my mother's constant plaguing. You know what a busybody she is."

He suspected it would not be polite to agree too wholeheartedly, so he made a noncommittal kind of noise in his throat.

She smoothed her dress over her knees in an unexpectedly self-conscious gesture. "Most of the time I am quite happy here, Avery. Things are better with the children, and you are always very kind to me."

Her smile was touched with a sadness that made him feel the uncomfortable urge to kiss her. "Of course we're kind to you. It was very good of you to come to us." He sounded too bluff, and he knew it. "What about everyone else? Have the neighbors been unkind? My family? I know Louisa—"

"No, no, everyone has been good to me. Especially considering I am a perfect stranger."

"Good." She *was* a perfect stranger, and so very unlike all of them, with her direct ways and her peculiar mix of whimsy and practicality. He patted her shoulder in a manner so avuncular it made him cringe. "This arrangement has worked out quite well for everyone, I think."

It was a ridiculous thing to be saying to one's wife. But their union had never been billed as anything but a marriage of convenience. The heavy knot in his stomach was likely nothing other than the infamous pudding.

"Yes." Her voice was small. "This arrangement has worked out quite well."

She was looking down at the kittens rolling about at her feet in their clumsy games, but he could not take his eyes off her profile. It was strong and decisive, with nothing of Elizabeth's cameo delicacy. No, Gillian's was more like a marble bust of a fierce Roman goddess.

The silence was drawing him in, allowing rein to thoughts he should not have. There was something about this damned hayroom that made him forget all his resolutions. Something about being alone with her outside of the house filled with servants, children, and memories made him feel the strange ache that was almost like longing.

It occurred to him the conversation had died between them entirely, but he was afraid if he spoke, moved, or even thought, the real world would come flooding back to him.

She sighed again, and he realized her thoughts had not been running on any of the rather unchaste lines of his own. "Would you mind terribly if I leaned against you?"

"What?" He drew back, entirely bewildered by her suggestion.

She shrugged. "I just . . . just for a moment feel the need to lean against someone. There is no need to look so horrified, Avery. I will not throw myself at you."

"No, it isn't that . . . I . . . well, I . . ." His flustered protestations faded away. There was something rather nice about feeling the weight of her head against his shoulder. Louisa used to lean on him like that when they were young, back in the days when Edgecott was courting her and she did not know if she could accept him. He had told her then she would be a fool if she married someone for whom she had no deep affection. It was ironic he should be in the same situation now. But somehow he sensed it was not exactly the same.

He could feel Gillian's rhythmic breathing. She was not crying or clinging to him. She was just, well, leaning. Strangely, instead of the rather helpless feeling he had experienced when Elizabeth had clung to him in her fits of weeping, he felt strong. The idea that capable Gillian, dauntless Gillian, should choose his shoulder to lean on, gave him a rather pleasant sensation of power.

They sat there for a long time, his arm around her shoulders, his fingers toying with an untamable mahogany curl that had slipped its bonds and was corkscrewing off like the wild tail of sparks at a fireworks display. She drew back at last.

"There. I'm done. Thank you. I just needed to be close to someone."

"Just anyone?" He meant to say the words teasingly, but they came out a low caress. His arm curled around her neck and his fingers invaded the thick mass of curls at the back of her head.

She drew a sharp breath, but there was no mistaking the expression of desire that leaped into her eyes. "Do you wish to hear me say it?" she asked, smiling faintly. "That it must be you?"

His mouth was just above hers. "Yes."

She was the one who closed the space between them. Her lips were just as he remembered them, warm and yielding. Her body, somehow smaller, slighter than he had expected, arched toward him. She pulled away, her breath coming quickly through slightly parted lips. "Yes," she said. "It must be you."

He kissed her again, greedily. He felt as though

he was drunk or as though he was someone else entirely. How was it Gillian seemed to release this man inside him that he didn't know existed? His hands tangled in her hair, pulling it down with gentle insistence. "I wanted you from the moment I saw you," he murmured against her throat. "I wanted to do this."

Her eyes were dark with passion. "Yes," she said again. Somehow the word was all-encompassing.

"I don't want you to be just a mother to my children, Gillian." He kissed her once again, but gently this time. "I want you to be my wife."

She jerked back in the circle of his arms. "No, you don't have to do that. Not for my sake. I'm happy here, Avery, I really am. You don't have to bed me just to please me." She stopped, a somewhat annoyed expression crossing her face. "Why are you laughing at me?"

He *was* laughing. He felt young, uninhibited. For the first time in years, he felt free. "If you think that I would make love to you merely out of politeness . . ." He stifled a groan and found her mouth with his own again. "It isn't just to please you." He took her face between his hands and looked at her. "I want to."

She dropped her eyes in embarrassment, but she did not pull away. "Are you certain, Avery? For I know that you—"

He cut her off with a languid, seducing kiss that wilted her protests. "I'm certain."

Chapter Twelve

Gillian poured herself a cup of tea and then decided she could not drink it. She pushed a kipper around and around on her plate and watched her husband cut his ham into smaller and smaller pieces.

He cleared his throat. "What are you planning on doing today?"

She resisted the urge to reply impatiently that she had told him three times already this morning. "I am meeting with the schoolmaster in town about a governess for Jane."

What was wrong with them? It was as though last night had never happened. No, it was worse than that. Last night was so beautiful that the awkwardness this morning stood out in stark, horrible relief. She should have known he would regret it. She should have realized that once their passion was sated, Elizabeth would steal back into his head and reclaim him.

"Ah, yes," He gave up on the meat and began searching amongst the pots of jam and preserves on the table for the salt cellar. "Don't forget about the wren tonight."

"I won't." She wasn't likely to forget anything when they kept having this conversation over and over again.

He was trying. She could tell he was truly making an effort to act naturally. But it was painfully obvious that Avery, no matter what he said, no matter how passionately he had loved her last night, now regretted his decision to consummate their marriage.

She felt a rush of shame. She could tell herself it had nothing to do with her and that her husband was suffering from some vague, Elizabeth-related guilt, but it was hard not to feel as though he was personally rejecting her.

They had spent hours last night talking. There had been no awkwardness then. Why should it be that now they suddenly found they had nothing to say to each other?

He salted his eggs and then did not eat them. "It will be a nice evening. The wren is always enjoyable." The forced brightness in his voice was nearly painful to hear. "In most places, it is only the tenants and townspeople who celebrate it. We count ourselves fortunate indeed to be included."

"Oh yes. I'm looking forward to it." She smiled and nodded vacuously. "Yes, it will be most enjoyable."

She traced patterns in the butter on her toast while he stirred yet another spoonful of sugar into his tea.

He cleared his throat. "Louisa always makes a lovely spiced punch."

"Yes, she said she would. She said it was quite the family tradition." She broke the toast into five small pieces and arranged them evenly around the edge of her plate.

Avery took a swallow of tea, made a face of revulsion, and put down the cup. He smiled again with effort. "And the children always enjoy the music. I know Louisa has all the neighbors and relations from miles around coming to the house."

Gillian slowly mashed her fork into her eggs and watched the rather gruesome effect with disinterest. "Yes, I'm quite looking forward to it, myself." Any more of this and she would fling herself at him and strangle him. "I was thinking of stopping by Dr. Fitzgerald's house," she said casually.

His eyes met hers, instantly alarmed. "Why? Is something wrong with the children?"

"No, everything is fine. I just thought I would have him take a look at Katie's leg. She is trying so hard to walk upon it. A brace might—"

"You know what he'll tell you," Avery interrupted. "He'll tell you she's too weak, that you'll likely kill her if you tax her little body with a treatment like that. Perhaps later, when she's older and stronger."

She put down her fork. It was a strange kind of relief to be able to vent her frustration on a topic that was acceptable. "But it should happen *now*, while she's growing. It will straighten quite naturally and her muscles will develop properly. It shouldn't take more than a few years—"

He looked at her as though she had proposed severing his daughter's limb instead of bracing it. "You know how prone to illness she is. She is just getting over another head cold. Her constitution is not strong. I know you think otherwise because she seems so happy and outgoing, but she doesn't have the strength. I will not risk losing her, Gillian."

"I only wanted to *ask* him," she snapped. Did he think she hadn't given this matter every consideration?

Avery put down his silver with an impatient clatter. "Do as you please. I already know what he will tell you."

She threw her napkin on the table and pushed back her chair. Why was it so impossible for him to see reason on this subject? "You seem to have the impression I don't care what happens to her. I am aware of her illnesses, but I am a good deal more of the opinion that they come from being cooped up in a hot nursery all day with no fresh air. It's stifling up there, Avery.

"And you are fooling yourself if you think that keeping her incarcerated up there will keep her from infection," she continued, warming to the topic. "Bitsy has nine younger siblings. She goes home to her mother's house every week. I'm certain Katie has gone through every illness those children have."

She had stood up and was now pacing the room. It was freeing to give vent to the anger that had been building within her all morning. "Furthermore, contrary to your dire predictions, Katie did not get sick after our day of sledding."

Her husband was regarding her with narrowed eyes. "And therefore I know nothing about child care?" he asked, his voice heavy with sarcasm.

She sighed. "No, of course I did not mean that. I only mean that I do not think her health is as delicate as you do. I think she will be as hale and hearty as you could wish if only Mrs. Ahern would allow Bitsy to keep the windows open a bit when the weather is fine.''

He pushed back his own chair, but did not get up. "Forgive me for saying so, but I believe that Mrs. Ahern, mother of five, and Dr. Fitzgerald are considered by most to have more expert opinions than you.''

It was the first time she had seen him truly angry. His blue eyes were dangerously bright, but everything else about him was very still. Unlike her own family, who ranted and threw things when they fought, Avery merely seemed to grow more and more calm.

Somehow his serenity annoyed her further. "I want another doctor to see her." She spun around to face him. "A Dublin doctor or, better yet, a London one. An expert who will tell us if she is able to bear a treatment that will help her." She knew she was on dangerous ground, but she plunged ahead.

"Dr. Fitzgerald is hopelessly old fashioned. He specializes in nothing more than pandering to bored ladies who fancy themselves ill just to amuse themselves. He doesn't want to put Katie in a brace because he doesn't want to admit he knows nothing about such things.''

What did it matter if Avery hated her for saying it? He was determined to turn her out of his life anyway. He disliked confronting unpleasantness, and that included Jane's temper, Katie's illness, his sister's bullying, and, of course, Gillian herself.

Avery's stillness became even more pronounced. There was something almost ominous about it. "What makes you think that your fine London doctors will know more than Dr. Fitzgerald, who has known Katie since the day she was born?" he asked with chilling coolness.

She walked to his chair and looked down at him. "Because of your fears, you will deny your child a chance to walk." She knew it was emotional suicide. Avery, passionate and tender as he had been last night, had never felt more than a reluctant acceptance of her presence in his household. Now he rose to his feet and looked at her with an expression of utter loathing.

"And you, because of your ignorant meddling, will deny her the chance to live." He did not lift his voice, but the hatred in it hurt as much as if he had struck her.

"Avery." Her tone was reproachful. "How can you even say that?"

He looked down at her with eyes that were very cold in his pale face. Then, without saying another word, he swept her a stiff, formal bow and left the room.

For a few moments she sputtered at the door, all the witty and cutting retorts she wished she had said at last coming to her lips.

How could she ever have thought she cared for him? Last night in his arms, she had very nearly thought she was in love with him. "Oh, Gillian." She sat down in a chair, suddenly feeling terribly tired. "Sometimes you are so very stupid. Stupid, stupid, stupid-head."

Of course Avery was volatile on the subject of his youngest daughter. Hadn't he lost his beloved wife when she was born? Even if the risk to her health was tiny and the potential benefits virtually guaranteed, he would not jeopardize the last child Elizabeth had borne him. Perhaps it was short-sighted of him, but it was understandable. She wanted to run after him shouting that she loved Katie, too, that she would do anything to ensure that the child had everything in life that she herself could give her. But it wouldn't matter. Katie was not hers.

For a strange moment, she found herself annoyed with Elizabeth. How odd that Avery's first wife should pop into her head at that moment. "Well, it's her fault anyway," she muttered. "If she hadn't had the bad grace to die, none of us should be in this mess. Avery would be happy, the children would be happy . . . ."

Would she be happy? She tried to imagine the natural extension of her former life. Perhaps she would have married Lord Winn or Lord Stubblefield after all. Or someone else entirely. Perhaps—she screwed her face into an expression of intense skepticism—perhaps she would have been happy.

She picked up a knife and jabbed it into the plate of butter. "And neither one of those poor men would have been happy married to a harridan like me." They would, of course, have lived in a fashionable Mayfair town house, with the requisite box at the opera and five o'clock rides through Hyde Park. There would have been the inevitable shooting parties in the autumn and the Season in the spring. Perhaps she would have had children of her own eventually. How silly that she should picture those imaginary offspring looking like Jane, Emmet, and Katie.

"No, I wouldn't have married any of them. Everyone involved would have been miserable." She propped her chin on the heel of her hand and wrote her name in the butter with the tip of the knife. Gillian Avery. It had become who she was.

She couldn't imagine living any other life than the one she had chosen.

The dining room door opened. When she saw the butler, she realized she had been hoping it was Avery coming back.

"What is it?" she asked, trying to keep the irritation out of her voice.

"The mail arrived," Callaghan replied. He handed her three letters. She noted, with a feeling of sheepishness, that he was looking at the mangled plate of butter with an expression of domestic horror. She thanked him and then walked over to the window to read what he'd brought.

One from her mother. She quickly passed over it. It was likely to be filled with overwrought questions asking how she fared in this godforsaken country, why didn't she write, when was she coming to visit her poor, lonely mother? Didn't she care what happened to a woman whose only child had first disgraced her and then gone off to live at the ends of the earth? And had she heard that Julia Hartford had made the most brilliant match with an earl? Only think what she herself could have done if she had only set her mind to it!

There was time enough to read that one later. The second one was from Julia Hartford herself. Her old friend expressed trepidation about embarking on a marriage with a man nearly thirty years her senior. But at least the old earl was not gouty, so there was every hope they should rub along tolerably well. Gillian put down the letter and sighed. All in all, her own life was far more pleasant than one might have expected for someone who, with little enough money and beauty to start with, had intentionally squandered her reputation.

Her thoughts were again dragged to last night. More than just physically, for the first time she had felt emotionally close to Avery. His gentleness had been infused with a passion that thrilled her. She had never even known that there were such sensations to be experienced until Avery had patiently, insistently shown her.

Her attention was caught by the sound of a horse coming around the back of the house. It was Avery. He was muffled to the eyes against the sleety rain, and his horse plunged unhappily up the steep path. The land at the back of the house was unlandscaped, even neglected. Gillian rather liked walking among the overgrown hedges and brambles. But she knew very well the little path led only to the small plot of land behind the church where all the Averys were buried.

"Going to visit Elizabeth?" The bitterness in her voice surprised even herself. It made perfect sense. The poor man, his judgment clouded by desire, had forgotten himself last night, but now regretted everything. She crossed her arms and scowled out the window at his retreating form. She should feel sorry for him, she knew. It was neither fair nor rational to feel so angry. He had never misrepresented the fact that his heart would always belong to his first wife.

Until now it hadn't mattered. She leaned her forehead against the cool glass and watched a clear pool of warmth spread out in the frosty film that coated it. Until now, she had been happy enough to take second place, to share him. But last night, when she had held his full attention, she knew she was experiencing a shadowy reflection of what Elizabeth had possessed every day of her life. For a brief while, she had felt what it would be like to be loved by him.

She pushed herself away from the glass and sighed again. There was no competing with a beautiful, saintly, apparently perfect woman who had the added advantage of sparing Avery from the irritations and minor squalls of cohabitation by virtue of being dead.

"If I'm jealous of her, it is only because she had all the pleasures of getting those three little sprogs, while I have to deal with the raising of them." She slanted an annoyed glance out the window. But there was no point in pretending to fool herself. Last night had not changed everything. It had only been a glorious confirmation of what had been happening insidiously for months. She had fallen in love with her husband.

Chapter Thirteen

"You look near frozen, milord. It's clearing up, though. It will be a fine night for the wren, but it's cold enough now." Healy took the horse's reins and led the horse to be unsaddled and groomed. "You'll likely wish you'd stayed out in the freezing rain today, though." He grinned over his shoulder.

"Why do you say that?" Avery's ride out to the cemetery was usually calming, but today it had done nothing to soothe his ill temper.

"Oh, I'd say you'll know soon enough."

In no mood for games, he scowled at the groom and took himself off toward the house. Callaghan relieved him of his greatcoat with a look of vague trepidation. "What has happened?" Avery demanded.

"Ah, well, sir . . ." The butler cleared his throat. "No one is in any danger, and it will all blow over soon enough."

Avery's voice lowered dangerously. "What?"

The man's gray eyebrows rose further up his shiny head. "You see sir, if I had known earlier . . . that is . . . well . . ."

He brushed by the man, somewhat relieved to have a reason to vent his foul temper. Likely as not, Emmet had brought a bag of snow into the house or given the housemaid a box of woodlice to care for. "Gillian!" he shouted, stomping up the stairs to her room. Would she never manage to keep the children under control?

She looked up from her writing desk when he burst into her sitting room. "Hello, Avery. Did you have a pleasant ride?" There was a studied pleasantness to her tone.

"What has happened?"

She sighed and lifted her eyes to the ceiling. "The servants have made too much of it. It is merely between Jane and myself."

Her cool, rational voice exasperated him. How could he be righteously irate when she was so dashed calm? "Tell me what happened, Gillian," he growled.

She glanced back at the letter she was writing, put her pen back in the stand, and folded her hands. "Janie and I had words. I shall let her tell you yourself, but suffice it to say she was very angry with me."

"I'm sorry to say that this is nothing new." He strode across the room to the window, found the view of the distant purple hills dissatisfactory, and strode back. Why did everything have to be so difficult? He had married Gillian to make his life easier, not harder. First the wrangling over Katie's leg, and now Jane. It was partly Janie's fault. The girl had apparently inherited his own stubbornness, but really, everything his new wife did seemed to bring on disaster. "You rearranged the room," he noted suddenly.

"Yes. I thought it was time for a change."

Until now, she had been content to leave everything just as Elizabeth had left it. He had rarely ventured into his first wife's private chambers, but he was fairly certain they had not formerly contained a large, graceful writing desk, deep blue curtains, or, glimpsed through the half-open door to her bedroom, a bed with a tapestry atop the finials instead of a canopy. Elizabeth's taste had been strictly floral. "Where did you get that?" he demanded, indicating the strikingly bold portrait of one of his more rakish ancestors staring out of the newly papered wall.

"I found it in the attic," she replied, smiling fondly at it. "I like it."

He closed the door to the hallway, and immediately wished he hadn't. It seemed too intimate in here somehow. His eyes continued to be drawn to the bed in the other room. What tapestry had she chosen? Did she lie awake at night and look at it? He had the unsettling vision of them both in her bed, making up elaborate stories about the scene that hung above them, dim in the candlelight.

It was far too warm in here. Since he couldn't very well set the door ajar again, he satisfied himself by crossing his arms and scowling at her. "I did not come up here to discuss your changes in decor," he said, well aware he had brought up the subject.

Gillian drew a deep breath. "Jane was very angry with me, so she ran away."

"What?" It was a shouted exclamation more than a question.

"She only went to your sister's house. I've brought

her back, and she is in her room," she continued calmly. "The house is in quite an uproar over it, as you can imagine, as Janie was kicking and screaming, quite as though I was trying to murder her."

"You bodily dragged my daughter back from Louisa's house?" The relief he felt on hearing that Jane was safe was supplanted by anger. How dare his daughter behave so badly, and, more shockingly, how dare Gillian brutalize her like that?

"Avery," she chided. "Do stop looking at me as though I beat the poor creature. I sent Healy to follow her when she ran off, so I knew she was safe. I suppose I should have let her stay there until she wished to come home, but I received a rather frantic note from your sister's nursemaid saying that Louisa was not at home, Janie was making her cousins cry, and would I please send Bitsy to retrieve her."

"Why did *you* go?"

She rose to her feet, supporting herself on the back of the chair as though she were tired. "Because Bitsy was afraid. You know how Janie can get."

He did know. His daughter was too clever by half, and she knew very well that a well-placed fit of sulks would ensure that Bitsy gave her her way. But he had thought things were better lately.

"I'm trying, Avery; you know I am. Half the time you think I am heartless and the other half too indulgent."

When she raised her eyes to his, he saw there were dark circles beneath them. She looked exhausted. Then he remembered he had kept her up half the night making love to her. It seemed like a long time ago. He had wanted her so badly. He had needed her. The violence of that desire, now that it was gone, alarmed him.

"How is it that when I left everything was calm, but when I return, the entire household is in an uproar?" The rational part of his mind reminded him that things were actually a good deal better than they were in the days before Gillian arrived. Even Mrs. O'Connor had stopped threatening to leave. "All I ask for is dinners served on time, children washed, and for a little peace and quiet." Of course, hours of riding alone had given him neither peace nor quiet. He had returned from his trip to Elizabeth's grave with none of the serene melancholy that the visit used to afford him. Instead he felt cold, wet, and just as guilty as before.

"I always try to think what you would do in the situation," Gillian sighed. "Well, in any case, the damage is done, and I made the best decision I could. It wasn't the violent scene you seem to imagine. Regardless, Jane is in quite a pet, and I would like you to go with me to talk to her."

A faint noise outside the door gave him the excuse he needed to open it and relieve the tension her closeness wrought. Mrs. Ahern looked up at him with a surprised expression.

"Healy said you had just come in from the cold," she stammered. "I thought you might want tea."

"Yes, certainly." He waved her away, scowling, and watched with satisfaction as she scuttled down the hall. There was little enough hope of keeping the entire household from knowing he and Gillian were quarreling, but there was no need to make it easy for them.

"Well." He turned back to his wife, careful to leave the door open slightly. "What have you done with Janie? Locked her in her room?"

With visible effort, she refrained from rolling her eyes. "No. Nor did I tie her to her bed or beat her. I told her you and I would deal with her when you returned."

"And you are hoping I will back up your decision."

Her smile was freezing. "Really, Avery, I am well aware that in a competition with Jane for your affection, I am hardly likely to come out the winner. I am merely asking that you explain to her that running away is not the answer to her troubles."

The irony struck him hard in the stomach. Yes, he was one to be preaching about running away. His first disagreement with Gillian, and he had retreated behind anger and then ridden off for hours. He had been unable to admit that last night's passion had disturbed him, and so he had turned and run like a coward at the first excuse that presented itself.

His wife's strange golden eyes were upon him. Behind the irritation, behind the exhaustion, there was an expression of pleading.

"I'll go to her," he said gracelessly. Then, because she still stood there watching him, he stepped over and gave her an awkward pat on the shoulder. "We'll work everything out."

He shouldn't have done it. It was as though they were two magnets that, once close enough, pulled together of their own accord. Once he had touched her, he wanted more. He wanted to feel her body down the length of his. The effort required to pull away was almost painful. "And I'm certain we will have some explaining to do at Louisa's tonight as well. She's not likely to approve of any such histrionics on Janie's part."

Going to his sister's house to greet the wrenboys

was the last thing he wished to do. Perhaps Jane should not be allowed to go. He hated the thought of her missing it. He still held in his mind the vision of little Janie dancing on the lawn to the wild music. Janie, before she became so intractably difficult. Before she lost more than children should ever lose.

He satisfied his frustration with the unfairness of the world by turning away from his wife without another word, brushing rudely by Mrs. Ahern as she came in with the tea, and stomping up the stairs.

Gillian sank down into her chair again and stared at the empty doorway.

"Men are like that, your ladyship, if you don't mind me saying so." Mrs. Ahern shook her head and poured out a cup of tea for her.

She dragged herself with effort out of the mire of her thoughts. "Like what?"

"Temperamental."

"Are they?" Gillian accepted the cup and smiled slightly. She and her housekeeper had finally reached a kind of peace. Mrs. Ahern begrudgingly admitted that Gillian's unorthodox organization of the linen closet made some kind of sense after all and that her menus were improving, and Gillian granted that Lady Edgecott's famous mustard plaster was superior even to her own mother's and had graciously conceded defeat in the kitchen. On the subject of Katie's health, they had a tacit agreement to disagree.

"You did the right thing with Miss Janie. She's getting too headstrong by far."

"I'm glad you think so." She wasn't at all certain

she had done the right thing. Dragging the girl back while she had writhed and screamed had been the most hideous experience she'd ever had. Of course, Jane had worked herself into a terrible temper, but it had been painful to listen to her high-pitched outpouring of hate. Little wonder Avery had looked at her with that expression of horrified disgust when he heard of the debacle.

It would have been comforting to confide in Mrs. Ahern, to ask her advice and confess her fears. But it wasn't the thing to be too familiar with the servants, and the housekeeper and she seemed to share very few views on the subject of raising children.

The muffled sound of raised voices came down the hallway. It sounded as though Avery wasn't faring much better with his daughter than anyone else.

Mrs. Ahern made a noise with her tongue against her teeth and started to gather the tea things together. "Shall I bring up her luncheon on a tray?" she asked, her head tilted to one side as she tried to catch the words to the shouted, one-sided conversation that wafted down the hall.

Angry footsteps thumped down two sets of stairs and the door to the study banged shut below her.

"Make up a tray, and I will take it up to her," Gillian said quietly.

Mrs. Ahern's brows rose, but she did not gainsay her employer. Gillian's gaze went back to the fire leaping about in the small grate.

It could not go on like this. She had thought she was strong enough to wait it out. She had hoped that at some point, the children would grow to accept her. Katie and Emmet sought her out now to beg for stories and for games of pretend in fortresses made of blankets draped over the nursery table. But the more they grew to love her, the more Jane seemed determined to reject her.

Mrs. Ahern had been dawdling, hoping to continue the conversation, but she turned at last and, again clicking her tongue, left the room.

Gillian looked down at the letter she had been writing. The lines were neat and even and the handwriting a clear copperplate, but the sentiments were as hysterical as Jane's had been. She begged her mother to let her come home. She couldn't live this way anymore. The constant resentment from Jane, the frigid distance from Avery . . . how could she tell her mother it hurt all the more to have felt, for one night, the joy of her husband's love, only to have it stripped away again?

Gillian read the note again and then, with an impassive gesture, threw it on the fire. "I could not bear to be away from him anyway," she said aloud, with a faint smile. Below her, she could faintly hear the creak of floorboards as he paced in his study.

There was a pause, and then the drawers of his desk banged open and shut several times. He would be looking for his pens, of course, not remembering she had arranged them in a vase next to the ink standish. In another moment he would be roaring to Callaghan to demand where he had hidden them. She smiled. She might be miserable with him, but there was certainly no chance of happiness without him.

Chapter Fourteen

By the time Avery had found his pens, bunched in an annoyingly pert bouquet in plain sight on his desk, he no longer felt like doing the accounts. He felt like having a nice, loud mill-down. If only George or Neil were about. His brothers were always good for a cathartic bout of pummeling.

Women. They were unfathomable from the start. Jane had started life as a sweet little bundle of giggles and spittle and ended up a foul-tempered hellion as impossible as he knew himself to be. Gillian, too, for all her quick wit and irresistibly ripe mouth, had an ability to drive him to hair-pulling distraction.

He found himself on his feet and pacing again. It was natural that he would find it upsetting. The well-being of his children might be at stake. He stopped and listened. The tense house was strangely silent.

He was being ridiculous. Gillian would never do anything to harm his children. She was patient long beyond the limits of his own endurance when it came to Katie's bedtime demands for just one more story or song. He had seen her tend gently to the inevitable results of Emmet's continual attempts to sever his own limbs, and every day he saw her politely rebuff Jane's sulks and rudeness.

He ran his hand through his hair and leaned against the study door. It was easier to vilify her. Otherwise, he would have to confront the memory of last night. She had felt right in his arms, and it scared him. The feeling of belonging, of satisfied need, was a warning shot to his psyche. Elizabeth could not be replaced. She should not be replaced. He would neither taint that beautiful memory nor risk ever going through the pain of such a loss again.

He untied Jane's skipping rope from between two chairs, coiled it up, and absently tucked it behind the mantel clock.

"I'm sorry, Gillian. I spoke hastily," he muttered. "You and I should talk with Jane together to ensure this does not happen again. Yes, that's a good phrase: I spoke hastily." He took another turn about the room and practiced again. "Gillian, we were both angry. I—no, you weren't angry at all, were you? You were cool as ice." He pulled at his collar and made a low growl in his throat. "I know Jane can be difficult, Gillian, but I know you did the best you could. Ah, that is just perfect."

He smiled at his reflection in the glass over the mantel and twitched his tumbled cravat into some semblance of order. He turned and nearly stepped on one of Katie's dolls. Yesterday, with Emmet's coaching, she had given the thing a rather lopsided

and scraggly haircut. He patted it fondly on the
head and set it on top of the pile of books Gillian
had been diligently rearranging.

"Yes," he told himself firmly, "best to get everything settled right away. Then we can be comfortable again."

She wasn't in her sitting room. The writing instruments at her desk had been neatly put away and
the fire banked. Still, he could not resist stepping
farther into the room. He wondered vaguely what
she had been writing when he came in before.
There was nothing in the little basket where she
usually kept letters for him to frank. A folded letter
lay on the desk, but it had the worn, dog-eared look
of an old piece of correspondence. He realized with
a start that it was his own handwriting marching
rigidly across it.

When had he ever written Gillian? He picked it
up and stared at it. The piece of paper had been
opened and refolded so many times that it nearly
pulled apart into pieces at the creases. The careful
wax seal was chipped and scarred in dozens of
places, but there was no doubt that it was his.

He sat down heavily in the spindly legged chair
behind her writing desk and frowned at the paper.
It was the letter he had written her in London to
propose to her. He felt his face heat with something
like embarrassment and shook his head. The words
were stilted, ridiculous. How could he ever have
written something so starched up?

Yet there were times when his words surprised
him. There was longing and hope. There was a
gentleness, almost an amorousness in his urging
her to accept his suit. Had he really written such
tripe?

She had told him once that the letter was the ntire reason she had accepted his suit.

Poor creature. She must have been sadly shocked o find that the man who had written this sweetly leading letter was cold and remote in person. She nust have discovered quickly that her husband was othing like what the gallant loops and turns of is handwriting implied. He wondered why she ad treasured it rather than thrown the thing on he fire.

The anger he felt was directed at himself. His leluded wife obviously held some hope that he eally was the man in the letter. For some reason is unruly mind took him back to last night. The ool who had written the letter had possessed him hen, too. He had held her and said all manner f foolish things. Like sugar on a toothache, the nemory was too sweet to bear.

He replaced the tattered letter on her desk and ooked about him guiltily. Where was Gillian, anyvay? Perhaps she was reading in her room or had lecided to lie down for a bit. The thought of coming upon her while she slept sent an unsettling vash of desire through him.

He craned his neck to look through the partly pened bedroom door, but the bed was empty. eeling vaguely like a spy, he silently shut the door o the hallway and slunk into the inner chamber. t was his house, after all. Besides, most husbands ad been in their wives' bedrooms countless times.

The room was a rich temple of blues and greens. The heavy drapes Elizabeth had kept closed to teep out harmful drafts were looped back, and the vinter sunlight lit a bright square on the floor. His wife did not appear to own many things. Her Iressing table was spartan compared to the many pots and bottles that adorned every surface in the rooms of his mother and sisters.

He made himself wait until last to examine the bed. It was a funny, makeshift arrangement with the tapestry tied to the posts of the bed with broad blue-gray ribbons at the corners. It bowed in the center slightly, but the effect was rather good. It was a hunting scene. A stag was preparing to leap out of the right side of the picture, while an entourage of highly unsuitably dressed courtiers trailed after it. The rich, soothing colors of the work complemented the rest of the room. He ignored the temptation to lie on the bed and experience what she must see every night before going to sleep.

His glance roved again around the eclectic collection of pictures she had chosen from the house's disused store and the vase of purple heather that sat on the mantel. More threatening than the ephemeral pleasure of desire was the dawning suspicion that his wife might be an interesting person. She had thoughts and preferences and perhaps even a whole philosophy of life he knew nothing about. His fascination with her beauty and appreciation of her good-humored wit might be no more than a dangerous beginning.

He gave himself a shake. This was dangerous indeed. Gillian could walk in any moment and demand to know what he was doing, poking around amongst her things. And he would probably slide his arm around her waist and kiss her until she drew him to the bed and let him make love to her again.

He could not afford to think about such things when there was a more emergent question at hand, the one of what was to be done with Jane. At the moment he was in favor of sending the girl off o an extremely strict boarding school. He never should have faced the viper-tongued creature alone. As Gillian had suggested, they should have done it together. He strode out of the room, careful to touch nothing.

He was steeling himself for another round with his daughter when he saw his wife making her way up the stairs to the nursery. She carried a tray that obviously contained his daughter's luncheon. A glimpse of her face showed her to be girded for battle.

All the lurking about must have gotten into his blood, for he waited until she had walked along the passageway toward Jane's room before he followed her up the stairs.

"Jane?" Gillian propped the tray against the doorframe to free her hand so she could rap with one knuckle on the door. "I've brought up your luncheon."

Avery slipped into the open door of Emmet's room. He was surprised to see Bitsy had made a pallet on the floor in here for his youngest daughter. Usually Jane and Katie shared a room, but he suspected the young woman hadn't had any desire to face the wrath of Jane when it was time to put Katie down for her nap. The little girl lay asleep on her makeshift bed, surrounded by Emmet's wooden cannons, tin soldiers, and beached ships. With her thumb in her mouth, she looked peacefully oblivious to the chaos around her.

"Let me in, Janie. I need to speak with you." Gillian's voice was calm but firm.

He couldn't quite make out Jane's shouted response, but he felt certain it contained several words he would have liked to know where she learned.

There was a rattle as Gillian set down the tray. "I know you're angry," she said. "And you are probably afraid, since you know you will be punished for running away and upsetting your father, your cousins, your aunt, and me."

Silence. Avery wondered what Janie was doing. Was she hiding under the blankets of her bed, shutting out Gillian's gentle, insistent voice? Or was she right on the other side of the door, her hand on the knob, considering whether she should open it?

"Yes, I know you are unhappy here," she said, evidently in response to Jane. "What would make you feel better?"

That was a question he had not thought to ask the girl. He had merely shouted at her for disobeying Gillian, ordered her never to behave so again, and, frustrated with his daughter's lack of response beyond a sullen glare, he had stomped off to let her pout in peace.

He peeked around the doorframe with one eye. Gillian was standing with her forehead resting against the closed door, listening to the voice within. A strange smile played across her lips.

"I don't believe that will happen," she said in a serious voice. "Even if it would make you, your father, and everyone else happier, it is very difficult to end a marriage once it is begun."

Avery forced himself to keep from leaping into the hallway bellowing that it would definitely not make him happier if she were to leave.

Gillian's smile had vanished. "Would you be happier living with your cousins? We would be very sad if you chose to live with your aunt, but I know you must be lonely here sometimes, and you are very fond of Fiona—" She paused, listening. "Well, perhaps you and Fiona will patch up your quarrel. In any case, if you are truly not happy here, I will talk to your father about another arrangement." She knelt down to the level where Jane must be standing on the other side of the door. "But you must think about it a long time. You cannot be running away from here or Aunt Louisa's house or Grandmama's house or any of the aunts' houses every time you are cross with someone."

Avery felt a strange tightening in his chest. How could Jane resist the sweet urging in her voice? Despite the fact that his daughter had always been unpleasant to her and had humiliated her by running away, Gillian cared so obviously for the child's happiness. How could she not throw open the door, fling herself into his wife's arms, and beg to be forgiven and loved?

Gillian sat for a long time, listening through the door as Jane's muffled voice rose and fell. "Of course your father would come to see you. He loves you so much, Janie. He brought me here to take care of you because he thought it would make you happier, not because he didn't care anymore."

Her hands were pressed flat against the door, as though she wanted to push through to the girl inside. Then her face jerked back, with a look of pain. "No, I don't believe it is that way at all." She thought for a moment. "Your papa will always have a love inside him for your mama. Nothing will ever change that. Just like he will always love you and Emmet and Katie. He brought me here to make things better for you, not because he'd stopped loving your mama or stopped caring about you."

The sense of relief he should have felt in hearing that she knew, entirely, why he married her and how he felt about Elizabeth did not surface. Instead he felt the familiar sense of guilt rising in his throat and threatening to choke him. Last night he had not been thinking of the children. And he certainly had not been thinking of Elizabeth. He had been thinking only of Gillian and how to bring that expression of blissful adoration to her face again.

Even today at the graveyard, he had had trouble remembering the sound of Elizabeth's voice or if they had ever laughed together late at night after they had made love.

"Janie." Gillian caressed the door with the back of her hand. "Please open the door. I would feel much better if we could talk face to face."

She waited, listening, then sighed. "No, I'm afraid I am not sorry for dragging you back. I couldn't let you go on bullying your cousins and putting Aunt Louisa's house into an uproar. Your papa agrees with me." He saw her look up to the ceiling with a wincing expression of contrition. But she must know it wouldn't do to tell the girl her papa had called his new wife a cruel monster for what she had done. And, in the light of calm reason, he saw why she had done it. If it had been him, Janie would have suffered much worse treatment.

"Yes, I'm afraid so. What kind of punishment do you think would be appropriate?" She waited for Jane's answer. "That's a start, certainly. I also think you might apologize to your cousins. What if we also agreed that we will take a little walk every day, just you and me?"

There was little doubt as to the tone of Jane's reply.

"Well, that way we could talk about what makes you angry and what you like and perhaps we can grow to like each other better," she went on, talking to the door with an anxious expression. "It will be very grown-up—two ladies taking a walk in the hedges without any interruption from the younger ones. We could have Mrs. Ahern bring us tea in the arbor. Can we try that?''

The disappointment on Gillian's face cut right into his heart. She got tiredly to her feet. "Well, think about it anyway. Your luncheon is getting cold out here. You should eat it soon. I feel certain Mrs. O'Connor made something nice for you. And you must rest if you want to go to your aunt's house to see the wrenboys tonight.''

Avery stepped back into the shadows of the room and prayed Gillian didn't stop in to check on Katie on her way downstairs. But she only paused in the doorway to make certain the girl was sleeping soundly and that the fire in the hearth had not gone out, then continued down the hall. He watched her retreat, her steps slow and her head down. In all her time here, she had never shown weakness. She had never shown anything but an unwavering determination to persevere. Now she looked tired, almost frail in her defeat.

A faint noise behind him made him turn. Jane's door opened slowly and two little arms reached out for the tray. He had almost condemned his daughter as impossibly hard-hearted when a suspicious sniffle gave her away. Gillian's words had touched her after all.

The pain in his chest grew stronger. He wanted to grab Janie and hug her and promise that things would be good again, and he wanted to run down the hall after Gillian. He would drag her to him and kiss her. He needed to make her understand that what she had done was brave and wise and kind and that he was proud he had chosen such a remarkable woman for the unenviable role he had offered her.

But he could do neither. Neither his daughter nor his wife would appreciate his eavesdropping or meddling.

In the room next door he could hear the faint sound of Jane's quiet sobs. He knelt down beside where Katie lay on her pallet. "Come here, sweet Kate," he whispered, lifting her up and draping her over his shoulder. She wiggled against him and then sighed back into sleep. He inhaled the baby smell of her white-gold curls in a sigh of his own. "I'm afraid at the moment you're the only female in the house who will let me hold her."

Chapter Fifteen

"Do you think we were right to let Jane come with us?" Gillian asked as she allowed Avery to hand her out of the carriage in front of Louisa's house. Was it her imagination, or did he hold her hand longer than was necessary for politeness?

"Yes. Though I don't know if her cousins will agree with us." He gave her a wry smile. "I think we are more likely to be chastised for bringing Kate with us."

She had never heard him refer to them together as we. It brought a strange, warm ache to her chest. After their quarrel this morning and the unpleasantness over Jane, he had been trying particularly hard to be congenial. She felt tentatively optimistic. Perhaps his anger had blown over.

She looked over to where Bitsy was struggling to convince Katie to keep her mittens on her hands and the ends of her scarf out of her mouth. "I will not be drawn into that argument with you again, Avery.'' She gave him a good-natured scowl. ''Your sister said expressly that none of the children who are coming have been ill. Only Anne's George has a bit of a cold, and he is staying home.'' She took his arm, and they walked up the steps together. ''And we will make certain she does not stay up too late.''

''You are here at last,'' Edgecott bellowed, opening the door so Jane and Emmet could race in. ''We've quite a crowd this year. It may be freezing, but at least it's dry, which is a good deal more than you could say last year, or even this morning for that matter. Peppering down, it was. I haven't seen anything like it in years. Nasty, slushy stuff. But now dry as you please. Don't mind the cold so much when it's dry.''

He ushered them in to a house stifling with heat, neighbors, and relations. Gillian once again found herself overwhelmed with the number of children running about. Some of them she hadn't seen since her wedding day. At least with the children, she had a chance of being correct at least a reasonable portion of the time if she called them all George. With the adults, she had no such hope.

Louisa looked up from where she was straightening the coat of one of her children. ''Oh, it's you. We thought perhaps it was a group of wrenboys. We already had one, you know. Children from the village, mostly.''

Her eyes were drawn to something across the room. ''Is that Jane?'' The lines at the side of her mouth deepened. ''Really, after her behavior today, I am surprised you would let her come. I heard about the debacle and I must say I'm not surprised. You are far too lenient with her, Prescott.

I will not tell you what she called my George, here. The unmanageable creature shut Regina and William in the cupboard for over an hour. She actually hit Fiona in the eye. Can you imagine? Just because the girl said that you have pretty curls, Lady Avery. Really.'' Louisa's eyes, so like her brother's, were coldly censorious. ''The girl grows wilder every day.''

Gillian felt a flush creep up her neck. ''I am so sorry. I had no idea she—''

''We talked about it, and Jane is very sorry for what happened today.'' Avery put his hand possessively on the back of Gillian's waist. She luxuriated in the feeling. Again he had said 'we,' just as though they were a real family.

Her husband narrowed his eyes meaningfully and beckoned to his daughter, who was kneeling in the window seat with her erstwhile enemy, Fiona, watching for the wrenboys.

Jane slunk over and stood in front of her aunt, her head down. ''I'm very sorry for what happened today,'' she said to the floor. ''It will not happen again. I will apologize to my cousins immediately.''

''Very well, Jane,'' Louisa said with a cold bow of her head. When the girl had scampered off, she turned back to her brother. ''Really, Prescott, she's become uncontrollable. I don't know what to think. She was such a sweet girl when Elizabeth was alive.''

''She's going through a bit of a difficult period.'' Though he waved his hand dismissively, Gillian heard the tension in his voice.

''Of course. I'm sure she feels her mother's loss keenly.''

''I think we will learn to manage tolerably well,'' Gillian replied with a bright, stiff smile.

Avery was staring into space with a faraway look somewhere between anxiety and sorrow. She recognized the expression. It pinched his face whenever he was thinking of Elizabeth. She was rather glad when a loud shriek from Katie drew her attention.

She excused herself and went over to extract the child from underneath a table. "What happened, my dear? Did you try to stand up under it?" She kissed Katie on the top of her flaxen curls.

"The poor creature lost her balance," a young woman volunteered. Gillian recognized her as the young, new wife of Avery's brother Neil. They had been married shortly after she and Avery had.

"At least she tries to stand now. Her twisted foot has kept her from walking thus far, but in the last few weeks she has shown an effort to try standing," she said, setting the wiggly child back onto the floor.

"Oh," the girl said sadly. "She is lame. And what a shame for such a pretty, sweet-tempered girl."

Gillian found herself struggling not to shout, as Emmet had, that they liked Katie the way she was. "It does not bother us, and it does not seem to bother her," she replied, with a jerk of her chin.

The girl's eyes widened. "Oh, I didn't mean any offense. I only meant . . ." Her voice trailed off into a confused mumble.

"I know," Gillian sighed. "Now she knows no differently. But how much harder it will be for her when she learns she cannot run and play like her brother and sister."

They watched Kate as she tried to bite off a gilded lion's head at the table's corner.

"Have you not seen a doctor about it?"

With heroic strength, Gillian kept from rolling her eyes. It would not do to express her frustration with Avery's resistance to seeking medical advice to this perfect stranger. "We are anxious that her health is too frail for any treatment," she said carefully.

A dark-haired toddler who might have been Sarah's little Horatio careened into Katie. Katie relieved him of the brocade sofa cushion he had been carrying and began cheerfully beating him over the head with it.

"She isn't as robust as she looks," Gillian said weakly, removing the weapon from the squealing, rosy-cheeked child.

"I hear Dr. Webster in Dublin is very good with such things," the girl said thoughtfully. "I have a friend from school who went to him after she broke her hip in a fall from a horse. I know your daughter's malady is not quite the same thing, but Dr. Webster specializes in the lower extremities."

It was hard to know what to think. Gillian smoothed her hand over the cushion, pretending to examine its intricate pattern. Should she steel her heart against fresh hope? But if she never had anyone other than old Dr. Fitzgerald look at the girl, she would always wonder if another doctor could have done something for her.

Katie crawled after the cushion, and when she came to Gillian's knee, she pulled herself up on her skirts. "Up, Gilly, up!" she demanded.

"Up you go." She swung the child into her lap and then turned her attention back to Neil's wife. "Perhaps I will write to him and ask if he thinks he could help," she said, disguising the anxiety she felt. Avery would never agree to it, and she couldn't very well force him to have his daughter treated. "Dublin is a long way away."

The woman stroked a finger across Katie's

chubby cheek. "She is a lovely child. I did not mean to meddle."

"Selina!" Neil reeled over and collapsed onto the sofa between them. "I see you've met Prescott's wife. Nattering over here like a pair of birds. Gossiping about what it is like to be married into the enormous Avery clan, no doubt. I daresay it is a bit overwhelming with everyone here." He turned to Gillian and grinned. "Selina is always saying she can't keep all the cousins straight."

"It would help if everyone had not insisted on either marrying or birthing someone named John or George," Gillian said, her smile rueful.

"Very much so." Neil laughed. "Demmed confusing. Perhaps I should teach a class in it."

His wife smiled. "I think I could draw family trees for months on end and still not have it straight."

Katie launched herself into her uncle's lap. Gillian tried to retrieve her, but Neil seemed entirely used to being mauled by small children. Katie, well acquainted with the contents of his waistcoat pockets, pulled out his pocket watch and began chewing on it.

"She is adorable," Selina said, evidently charmed by the long strand of drool attaching Katie to her husband's trousers. "And such pretty curls. She must get them from you."

She felt a strange shock. "Oh, I'm not—"

"Gillian ain't this sprog's mother," Neil broke in. "The mother of Prescott's children died, oh, over two years ago now."

"I'm sorry," Selina said. "I didn't know."

Neil detached Katie's sticky fingers from their grip in his hair. "Told you she couldn't keep it straight." He turned to Gillian. "You're nothing like Elizabeth," he said suddenly.

She felt her smile stiffen. "I'm afraid her memory is a lot to live up to," she said. That was certainly a grand piece of understatement. No one could possibly know how keenly she felt the difference between them.

"I was just telling Prescott how you and she were about as different as two women could be. Now Elizabeth was a fine woman, and I know Prescott and she were childhood sweethearts ..." He allowed Katie to crawl over to Selina's lap, where she showed a violent desire to pull off the buttons that adorned that woman's bodice. "But you've a damned sight more spirit. Louisa told me about you dragging off poor Janie. It's about time someone took her in hand. Janie, I mean, not Louisa. Though"—he laughed—"someone ought to take Louisa in hand as well. Turning into Mama, she is."

What was the fool thinking, comparing her to Elizabeth? There wasn't a minute of the day Avery didn't do so, of course, but the last thing he needed was to have everyone else reminding him of her own vast shortcomings. She tried to find her husband in the crowd, but he was nowhere to be seen.

"I told him it was about time he got married again," Neil said proudly. "No disrespect to Lizzy, but a man can't stay celibate forever." He gave her a conspiratorial nudge in the ribs. "You can always hire a nursemaid to raise the sprogs, but a man needs someone in his bed. And Avery isn't the type to take a mistre—"

"That's quite enough, Neil," Selina said in a sharp tone. "I think it would be best if we helped Louisa with the food and drink. The wrenboys will be here any moment, and she'll need someone to help out." With an apologetic look to Gillian, she returned Katie to her and dragged her husband up by the elbow.

Gillian held her smile as long as they were watching her, and then let it go. She saw Avery standing at the window with the children, watching for the appearance of the wrenboys. Though his back was to her, there was a change in every line of his body. He turned and smiled at her, but there was no warmth in it. The pleasant camaraderie that had sprung up briefly between them was gone.

What kind of nonsense had Neil been spouting? How like a man to bring up the marital act, and today of all days! She knew, of course, that everyone in the room assumed once they were wed they had consummated the union. How could they know that until last night he had remained faithful to Elizabeth?

Avery crossed the room to her. "They're coming up the road," he said, pleasantly. "Come, so you can see them." He took Katie from her arms and guided her over to the window. Though he was polite as always, the shield of cool reserve was firmly in place.

"Avery, I—"

He looked down at her, his eyes expressionless. "What?"

"Nothing." There was nothing to say, really. Certainly nothing that could be said here.

There was the sound of drumbeats in the distance. Then over the lawn came a strange group of people playing a jaunty march. They were dressed in white and wore sprigs of some kind of plant in their caps. Some were armed with flat drums, fiddles, and concertinas. The man in front carried aloft what seemed to be a bushy bouquet of greenery. The children in the window seat began squealing excitedly and ran to the door. The room quickly emptied out onto the front steps. Only Avery and Gillian were left.

"That's O'Rahilly's March they're playing," Avery volunteered. "They always play it when they walk from house to house."

She watched them for a moment as they made their way up to the house. "What a lively party they are. What is the drum they play with the paddle?"

"It's called a *bodhrán*. I suspect you recognize all the other instruments."

"Yes, but what is the man in front carrying?" She stepped closer to him to point to the man carrying the branch of greenery. She should use this time they had alone to tell him to take no notice of Neil. Why had the fool gone and spouted nonsense on tonight of all nights?

"It is a bunch of furze," he replied. "You know, from the song: *The wren, the wren, king of the birds, on St. Stephen's day was caught in the furze.*" He looked surprised at her blank expression. "No? Well I suppose it is a particularly Irish song."

"Prescott," she tried again. It felt strange using his Christian name, but since everyone else in his family called him by it, it seemed ridiculously formal to be the only one who didn't. "The last few days have been, well, eventful, and I just wanted—" She wasn't sure what she wanted. To assure him she understood if he wished to discontinue their marital relations? To beg him not to?

"Out. Out." Katie stretched her arms toward the crowd in the doorway.

Avery was looking at her, obviously waiting for her to continue.

"I just wanted . . ." It was hopeless. She didn't know what she wanted.

"Gillian, it has been a long and difficult day. We were both out of temper this morning and Jane's histrionics did nothing to improve matters. Let us pretend today did not happen and begin again tomorrow."

And last night, she wanted to ask, *did that happen?*

As if he had read her thoughts, he smiled in a bland way that was meant to be comforting. "Everything will be just as it was."

Chapter Sixteen

The wrenboys stood in a semicircle in front of
the steps. A tall, thin man Avery recognized as the
blacksmith began beating his *bodhrán*. In a sudden
jumble of sound, everyone else joined in. He recognized it, but there was something in the jaunty
embellishment that made it sound entirely new.
Marianne's infant set up an insulted roar at the
sound, and Katie looked a little frightened. He
bounced her in his arms in time to the tune. "Do
you like the music, my dear?"

"Loud," she said, an imperious frown crossing
her plump cheeks.

"Oh, but, Katie, it's dancing music." Gillian took
her hands and did a little skipping step in front of
her. Katie laughed at her. "Isn't it wonderful?
Ever so much more lively than the music they play
in London. How could anyone listen to this and
not want to dance?"

Avery found himself relieved that Katie was there, her usual, attention-demanding self. Otherwise, he would be standing alone with Gillian, expected to say something meaningful.

Why did it seem tonight everyone in his family was comparing Gillian to Elizabeth? It was inevitable, of course, but it made him all the more self-conscious of the awkwardness between them. They had only been married two months, he reminded himself. He had known Elizabeth all his life. It had taken only two months to break down his resolve not to bed her. The lump of guilt was heavy in his stomach.

The wrenboys finished the tune with a flourish and launched into another one. It was a waltz he had heard many times at the assembly in Newcastle West. It must have been years ago now. He hadn't been there since before Elizabeth died. Had they ever waltzed together? He felt a strange sense of panic when he realized he couldn't recall. As a married couple, it certainly would not have been frowned upon. Perhaps Elizabeth hadn't known how.

"Do you know how to waltz?" The question was out before he even knew it had formed in his head.

Gillian looked up in surprise from where she was pretending to bite off Katie's fingers. "Yes."

There was a stretch of agonizing silence. He knew he had made it sound as though he was about to ask her to dance. But he couldn't. There would be something very wrong about it.

"Would you like to waltz with me, Katie?" Gillian asked cheerfully. She held out her hands, and Avery let her take the child. In another moment his wife had slipped through the crowd in the doorway and was waltzing lightly in the space between his family and the musicians. Katie flung out her arms and let out a shrill squeal of enjoyment as they bobbed and whirled about.

Avery resisted the urge to push through everyone, grab her by the elbow, and apologize to his family that his wife was making a spectacle of herself. But before she had completed two revolutions, Selina had joined with Neil, and his brother-in-law Alan Scanlan swung his daughter into a sweepingly exaggerated waltz. His sister Anna pulled her husband out onto the makeshift dancefloor. Mr. Foley led his giggling wife out by the hand.

He thought of the time Janie and the other children had danced on the lawn. Then the adults had never even considered joining them. But this time no one seemed to think twice about the propriety of dancing out-of-doors. He looked for Janie now, but did not see her in the crowd.

The scene was strangely unreal, like watching fairies dance on the lawn. Mismatched in size and wildly varying in skill, the dancers whirled about in small vortexes of skirts and chubby limbs. He had a glimpse of Gillian's cheek pressed to Katie's as they laughed and spun until they staggered.

He smiled. Gillian was right. How could one keep from dancing to such music? Even Lord Needling was swaying back and forth in time to it. And it seemed the perfect place for it, with the cold, sharp air and the snow so bright it hardly seemed like nighttime. Perhaps it would even snow a bit before morning. The wrenboys sawed away, flushed with the energy of their playing. They would earn the coins and drink due to them tonight.

His mother brushed past him, muttering something about the catching of one's death. For a comical moment she pursued Gillian and Katie as they bounced across the lawn, then caught them and draped a wrap around the two of them. He could not catch her words, but he had a very good idea of which lecture she had chosen to recite. To his surprise Gillian handed Katie over to the woman, put her arms around them both and started them waltzing. She grinned and then turned to take the hands of Emmet, who had been studiously digging up grubs in the flowerbeds. Soon they were pendulously swinging back and forth to the time of the music.

He had never danced with Gillian, not even at their wedding. It had never even crossed his mind she might wish to do so. But watching her laugh as she tilted her chin to the stars and turned in time to the music, he wondered that she had never voiced a desire to attend the weekly assemblies in town or the innumerable rout parties thrown over the holiday season. She had seemed content to spend the evenings at home, reading to the children at bedtime and playing softly on the pianoforte while he wrote letters or read the paper.

What would it be like to take her hand and slide an arm around her slim waist? He pushed the thought from his mind.

"I see you are frowning," a voice at his side said.

"I was." He looked down at Louisa with a cool expression of condescension calculated to annoy her.

She shook her head, oblivious to his censure. "I agree. They look like the veriest fools. When we were young, the wrenboys came and played a few tunes, we gave them some money and a few bottles of whiskey, and were done with it." She flung out her hand in an expansive gesture. "There was none of this cavorting about like heathens."

Light from the house lit golden patches in the flowerbeds, but the gibbous moon had taken over the rest of the snowy world. It whitened the costumes of the wrenboys until they glowed even brighter than the pearly expanse of lawn. In the dark lake of dead grass cleared in front of the steps, the dancers wove in and out in a chaotic country dance he suspected his wife had invented on the spot.

"Dance with us, Papa!" Emmet reached out his hand to him as he spun by in Gillian's arms. He felt a momentary surge of panic and shook his head. It was better to be on the outside, watching. Joining in the impromptu festivities was not only beneath his dignity, it was somehow dangerous. Gillian would think . . . well, she would think something, anyway.

"They look like wild creatures," Louisa sniffed. "Like something out of one of those rather terrifying fairy tales our nurse used to tell us. It isn't at all the thing, Prescott."

"The children seem to enjoy it," he said mildly.

She gave a snort. "You do not see my children out there."

No, Louisa's children, still preternaturally tidy, stood on the steps, their mouths agape as they stared at the whirling scene.

"You would not have seen your Elizabeth conducting herself in such a manner."

"No."

"She was always a lady. I don't believe I ever saw her do anything beneath her station."

"Of course not."

His sister seemed dissatisfied by his bland agreement. She watched the dancers for a moment, her mouth compressed into a thin line of disapproval.

"I really do not know what to say to you, Prescott, except that I told you it would be so. Fancy marrying someone you'd never laid eyes on. It's absolutely medieval. Even if she is the daughter of Mama's dearest friend, you should not have taken it as a guarantee of her good breeding. Mama herself admitted that Evelyn Harwell was very much changed indeed. I must say, Prescott, I thought the woman shockingly high-handed. She acted as though we were all savages out here and that she was the only one who knew civilization. Most unpleasant." She leaned closer. "It is little surprise that the daughter of such a woman would be wild and unmanageable."

He would not be goaded into an argument with his sister. "On the contrary. She has always behaved most properly."

"Properly?" Louisa echoed in disbelief. Her hand stabbed stiffly toward the dancers. "I should hardly call this acting properly."

He leaned back against the doorframe and squinted up at the sky. There seemed to be a million stars on such a clear night. More stars than blackness in between them. "I see no harm in it."

"I see a great deal more harm in what has become of your children. Dragging Katie out on a night such as this! You know how delicate she is. She'll have an inflammation of the lungs before the New Year, I'll warrant."

"Mama has taken her inside and has put her to bed," he said. He tried to imagine what it would have been like if Elizabeth had been here this Christmas. There would have been the usual toys and their subsequent breakage. There would have been a pleasant meal with the children, unmarred by any smoking monstrosity of a Christmas pudding. There would have been no row with Janie, and certain no dancing on the lawn. It would have been like every other Christmas until he met Gillian.

"And Janie," his sister said, as though she read his thoughts. "Really, Prescott! When I heard what happened today I nearly dropped. Dragging the poor girl home like some criminal, when she had come to my house for sanctuary."

"I do not wish to discuss it." He wanted to go home. There was somehow too much beauty in the scene before him. The dancers revolved in and out of the half light to the leaping strains of music and the shrill laughs of the children. It seemed like dozens of them, dressed in their best clothes, were running about in packs like puppies. No, it was not right to get caught up in it. He needed to go home. To think about Elizabeth.

If he sifted through the collection of her things: the ring he had given her when she turned sixteen, a miniature painted when they were first betrothed, the little stitched baby gown she had embroidered so painstakingly while she was carrying Janie, then perhaps he could remember her face and her voice. Those were things he thought could never fade from his memory, and yet, damn his cursed inconstancy, he found it harder and harder to recall what they had done in the evenings or if she had preferred piquet to whist.

Instead a curly-haired Amazon kept invading his memories.

"Oh, dear, you all look so solemn."

He blinked and found that very person standing before him. Her cheeks were flushed with color and curls stood on end all around her head. He dropped his eyes from her vibrant beauty, feeling a sudden rush of desire and the inevitable second wave of guilt.

"I suppose I've been behaving with shocking lack of manners. But your George, Lady Edgecott, seemed to be having such a good time being spun about. He said he felt like he was flying."

Avery wondered if it was his imagination that he saw a spark of devilment in her eyes. She knew very well Louisa did not approve of unseemly conduct in her children and certainly would not have spun them about the lawn.

"Indeed." Louisa's smile was chilly.

"Lord Edgecott asked me to request that you serve the whiskey punch now. The poor musicians must be exhausted. They've certainly earned their keep tonight."

Louisa gestured to the servant with an annoyed flick of her wrist. She squinted into the darkness. "Edgecott is out there? Dancing?"

"Oh, yes," Gillian said with every appearance of gravity. "He took over the spinning of young George."

Louisa gave her a tight smile. "Well, it seems as though everyone has gone a little mad tonight. Indeed, while I always enjoy the wren, I think most of us prefer it not to degenerate into a romp. I'm afraid Edgecott was wrong in encouraging you. You have naturally high spirits, and I, of course, would never be one to dampen them, but I'm afraid the family's dignity will suffer." She drew a sharp breath and crossed her arms. "It will be all over town tomorrow that we were out on the lawn like pagans." She frowned down into the gathering.

"Don't be so stiff-necked, Louisa," Avery chided. "We've lived here for generations. Everyone knows we're a ramshackle lot. The parties thrown in Grandfather's day . . ."

"Indeed, we could afford to repair our good name." She looked down at Jane, who was standing in the shadows of the steps. "Jane, come here my poor dear. You must find all this confusion most disconcerting." She held out her hand to her niece.

"I don't find it so," said Janie. She came to her aunt's side, and looked calmly out over the scene.

"It must be most upsetting to see your stepmama dancing about like a wild thing."

Jane looked up, her pale eyes expressionless in the darkness. "On the contrary," she said in her cool, grown-up voice. "We like Gilly the way she is."

Chapter Seventeen

"Why did Papa marry you?" Jane asked suddenly. She stopped in the middle of the graveled walkway and turned to Gillian. "He didn't know you from before, did he?"

Gillian smiled. She shouldn't be surprised. Jane always seemed to ask the most penetrating questions on their daily walks. "No," she replied. "He didn't know me from before." After nearly a year of marriage, she still wasn't sure if she knew the answer to the first question.

Jane picked up a flame-colored leaf and spent a long moment affixing it into the buttonhole of her coat. "Grandmama and your mother were friends," she mused. "I find that hard to imagine."

Jane had had ample opportunity to observe Gillian's mother when they had gone to London for the Season. Avery was at the parliament houses all day, and had thus escaped the agonizing drone of her mother's continuous badgering. "They're both strong-minded women," she agreed ruefully. "Perhaps they have changed since they were schoolgirls, but they both always claim to be inordinately fond of each other. At least until they see each other again."

"It was very wicked of Emmet to set her morning room afire, I suppose, but it was much nicer once we had our own house in Town." She looked up at Gillian with an innocent expression. "Is it rude of me to say that I don't like her very much?"

Gillian took her hand and they continued down the path together. "Well, it would be rude if you said it to her in person. I must agree with you that the Season was much more pleasant once we were living in our own house." It had been very comfortable, really. Though she had grown up in London, she enjoyed taking the children to see the sights, and it had been so gratifying to see Avery come home every evening flushed with excitement at being involved again in government. She had been relieved to find that her true friends did not shun her acquaintance and the rest of the *ton* did not appear to have any recollection of the former, ruined Miss Harwell.

"Will we go again next year?"

"Yes, but this time I think we will have our own house from the start. Your papa will have to go to London every spring for the session."

Jane scuffed along the path in silence for a moment. "So why did you marry him?" she asked, returning to her original question.

Tenacious creature. She smiled fondly down at her. "Because he asked me to," she replied honestly. "And how could I have possibly said no to a man as perfect as your papa?"

She considered telling Janie about the letter Avery had written her in London. But how could she explain that his words had made her feel, for the first time in her life, needed? It was an explanation entirely too fanciful for someone of Jane's unromantic disposition. Too fanciful for her own unromantic disposition as well, she reminded herself.

Perhaps neither of them were perfect, but things with Avery had certainly improved in the last eight months. While he was never particularly open or passionate, he was pleasant and caring. One couldn't ask for more, really.

"Here is Katie," Jane said with a worldly sigh. "At least Bitsy made her wait until the end of our walk."

She hugged Avery's oldest daughter around the shoulders. It touched her to see how jealously Jane guarded their private time together.

"I'm telling!" Katie announced shrilly over her shoulder. She thumped erratically down the pathway on her crutch and skidded to a stop in front of them. "Emmet said is not my birthday!" she cried, hopping about like a little mechanical toy.

Gillian swooped down and caught the little girl around her waist. "Well, it isn't."

"It is!" Katie tried to look annoyed, but could not help giggling as Gillian lifted her high in the air. "It is. Papa said so."

She brushed the flaxen hair out of the girl's eyes. "Your birthday was two days ago. And how old are you?"

Katie paused and carefully arranged her hand. "Tree," she announced confidently, showing four chubby fingers.

"And what did you do on your birthday?"

The girl's small mouth puckered in thought. "Wore princess dress and ate cake. I wants birthday today. I wants cake. No cake for Emmet, though. He very bold."

"Well, we'll see how Mrs. O'Connor feels about cake again today. Besides, Emmet gave you a very nice present for your birthday. Your new doll, Molly, remember? Perhaps we'd better let him have some cake." She set Katie down and handed her her crutch. "We have something special planned for today. Do you remember?"

Katie thought for a moment. "Going to Janie and Emmet's mama's grave."

"She was your mama, too, of course," Jane put in.

The girl's pale brows drew together. "Gilly my mama."

Gillian laughed and set the girl's bonnet straight. "No, I'm not. Your mama—"

"Is in heaven," Katie finished for her. She lay her crutch across two stone garden urns and swung by her arms from it. "Emmet said I kilded his mama."

Gillian sat down on a wooden bench and leaned over to speak to the girl. "Emmet is wrong," she said firmly. "I hope you told him so."

"No." Katie sighed. "I bited him."

At that moment the recipient of this ill treatment bounded across the lawn. "Gilly, Mrs. O'Connor said that the packed luncheon is ready." He saw his sister and instantly set up a loud wail. "And Katie pinched me."

"I didn't," Katie said serenely from where she still swung from her crutch. "I bited you."

Gillian got up and smoothed her gown. "Katie, we can't go about biting people, no matter how much we would like to. And, Emmet, if you taunt your sister to violence, I can't be expected to show you too much sympathy." She herded them toward the house. "Jane, will you see that everyone has hats and coats while I get the lunch?"

The four of them set off through the spinney at the back of the house. It was a fine late summer day. The sun slanted down through the trees and lit ragged patches in the brambles along the path. Emmet ran ahead to check on the horse chestnuts he was stockpiling in the hollow tree. The weather all summer had been indifferent, but it was warm today, and the girls took off their bonnets and swung them by their ribbons as they laughed and chattered.

The path was familiar to them all now. There was the place Emmet had sprained his wrist when he fell out of the tree, the place where Katie had been stung by a bee, and the clearing with the perfectly round stone in the middle that Jane said Papa said was from the druids. At the creek they stepped across the little dam they had built and stopped to admire the Home for Orphaned and Indigent Slugs they had constructed together the day before.

At last they reached the top of the hill where, on the right hand side, lay the house. Directly in front of them was a gentle slope down to the St. Colman's church. It was a peaceful place, too difficult to get to for most of the townspeople. She often came here with the children to play and watch the world go on below them. She did not like to admit that she always watched the churchyard for Avery.

"Where is Papa?" Jane asked as she helped Gillian lay out the cloth at the flattest part of the hill.

"I don't know," Gillian replied with the cheerful air of fond unconcern she had mastered. Her husband had ridden off that morning without a word to her. In the past months they had come to a kind of understanding. They still tucked the children into bed together and spent the evenings in quiet companionship. He even consented to come to her bed on occasion, though he always slipped away in the dark afterward without a word. But for the most part, he made it clear that he was happiest when she did not intrude upon his life overmuch or prod too deeply into his psyche.

"It is a sad time for him right now. He still misses your mother a good deal. This is the time of year he remembers her most."

Janie continued to carefully unpack the ludicrous amount of food Mrs. O'Connor had sent with them. She appeared to be deeply in thought for quite a long time. "Will he always be sad about it?" she asked at last.

"Of course. She was very special to him." She kept her voice intentionally neutral. "But as time goes on, he will feel better." How could she tell the children otherwise? She could not tell them she feared he would always look at them with that hungry expression, as though he was looking for Elizabeth's resemblance in their faces, and that he would always look at her as though he were somewhat alarmed to find a strange woman still living in his house.

"Gilly, Emmet won't let me hold flowers."

"She was holding them too tight and they were going to break," Emmet insisted, holding the garland of late roses above his little sister's head.

"I wants to take flowers down now," Katie objected, her voice dangerously near a whine. "I wants to take flowers down to Mama's grave now."

"I think we should wait until after our luncheon," Janie said primly.

"Now." Katie crossed her arms over her crutch. "I's birthday girl, Janie. I wants it now."

"You're being a spoiled baby. And you're not the birthday girl anymore. Your birthday was days ago. *My* birthday is next so we have to do what *I* want."

Gillian leaned back on her hands and smiled. There was a time when she would have cringed to hear them squabble so. Now it just seemed so much a part of their everyday life that she hardly noticed it. Avery said she was a Rousseauian philosopher, allowing the children to work out their differences with all the civility of wild piglets, but she always reminded him serenely that there had not been a single goldfish in the teapot since the first day she arrived.

The children had finally decided they would eat their luncheon and then would take the flowers down to the grave before they savaged Mrs. O'Connor's plum cake.

Yes, matters had improved between Gillian and her husband. It had been a slow process, certainly, but they had a comfortable existence these days. It was no more passionless than the Edgecotts' marriage, or the Foleys', or the Harveys'. And there were certainly times, like when Avery had taken them all to the horse races last March and when he had taught the children to swim in the pond in the summer, when she had honestly thought herself the happiest person in the world. He was not the husband-prince of her childhood dreams, but it was indeed a comfortable existence.

"Papa!" Emmet shrieked. "There is Papa!" He pointed down the hill.

She was not wholly surprised. Though she never pointed him out to the children, she had seen him there many times over the summer. She always averted her eyes when she saw him, though, and busied herself with other matters. She felt guilty, as though she was spying on his private assignations with Elizabeth.

Avery dismounted on the far side of the church-yard and let himself in by the gate. He looked up in surprise when he saw the three children galloping down the hill toward him. Janie wore the garland of roses around her neck like a Newmarket winner. Katie, her crutch working furiously, trailed far behind them. Gillian felt a painful knot form in her chest. If only something could be done for the girl.

She was tempted to go down with them, but decided at the last moment to leave them alone. Down the hill, she could see Emmet jumping from one foot to the other, chattering away. She could see from his gestures toward the flowers and the gravestone in the corner that he was explaining their mission.

Avery looked up the hill toward her, but the expression on his face was impossible to read at this distance. Perhaps he condemned her for interfering, or was merely surprised that she would put herself to the trouble of arranging this outing.

He swung Katie onto his shoulders and took Emmet by the hand. Janie followed as they walked over to the corner of the churchyard where Eliza-beth was buried. Gillian lay back on the grass and stared at the clouds. She pretended, while she blinked away the sudden prickly feeling behind her eyelids, that she was giving them privacy to commemorate their loss, but she knew it was self-deception. In truth, she could not bear to see them bunched together in that corner of the churchyard, united as a family, without her.

"Better to be on the outside looking in than to never have lived to see those children grow up," she told herself.

But a sulky voice inside her reminded her that there had been plenty of nights she thought she would happily have exchanged Elizabeth's brief life as the center of Avery's bright universe with her own role as a minor satellite.

A squirrel loped along on the branch above her and scolded down at her. "I am just like Katie," she muttered. "Jealous of any toy anyone else has. Why can I not be satisfied with things the way they are? I've a much better life here than I would have had in London."

"London?"

She sat up to see that Avery and his children had come up the hill together to finish their luncheon.

"What did you say about London?"

She smiled weakly. "I was just talking to myself." She found herself unexpectedly tongue-tied. She shoved a plate toward him. "Would you like some plum cake?"

The children dragged him down before he could make any excuse. "I see you have quite a feast here," he said pleasantly.

"Gilly says we should connemeremerate Mama today on account of today being like her birthday, only it is the day she died," Emmet spoke up confidently.

Gillian busied herself with searching the basket for a knife to cut the cake. "It seemed like the correct thing to do, Avery. I hope you're not cross that I didn't discuss it with you.''

"It was very good of you to do anything at all," he said in a low voice.

She met his eyes for a moment, then was forced to drop her gaze again. "Well, of course. I know you always did before."

Avery looked at her with a peculiar expression. "But *you* didn't have to—"

Emmet threw himself onto his father's back and begged to be galloped about. Avery gave her an apologetic smile and then got up to comply with his son's demands. For the next half hour there was no conversation but that relating to horsey rides, birthday presents, and whether Emmet or Katie had the largest piece of plum cake.

Avery flung himself onto the grass and pulled over his half-empty plate. "Look, Janie, there's a hare." He pointed with his fork at a leggy ball of fur that was lumphing casually across the grass. "If you are very quiet, and creep, oh, so slowly up to him, you might be able to catch him."

"I wants hare," Katie announced. "My hare."

"Be quiet, Katie. You'll frighten him," Emmet chided her. He got to his feet and began to follow the animal as it nibbled its way through the undergrowth.

"He mine, Emmet.

"It will likely take all three of you to catch him," Avery said with a faint smile. "Go on. But make certain you are very quiet. If you catch him, we will build a little house for him."

Gillian watched the children tiptoe after the hare. Mercifully, it seemed merely wary of the line of the giggling and quarreling hunters who followed it. She turned back to her husband. "Why did you send them off on such an errand?"

He was looking at her with a thoughtful expression, but he merely shrugged.

It was ridiculous that she should feel shy after nearly an entire year of marriage to this man, but she found herself searching her mind rather frantically for a topic of conversation as the silence grew longer.

"What you've done for the children today was very kind," he said at last.

"I'm sorry I didn't discuss it with you, Avery. I should have, but I didn't think of it until this morning, and you were already gone." She brushed a few crumbs off the cloth they sat on. "I do hope you aren't annoyed about it. I should have made more of an effort to include you, I know."

"Not at all. I perhaps should not have invaded your party. But I came out here as soon as I heard you were here."

She looked up at him, but he was watching the tops of the children's heads as they bobbed through the underbrush. Hadn't he planned on coming out to Elizabeth's grave anyway? He could not possibly have forgotten such an important day.

"There is something I wish to discuss with you."

"Yes?" She tried not to reveal that her heart had begun to pound rather heavily at his grim expression.

He pulled a letter from his pocket. She recognized the seal and her heart sank. "It is from a Dr. Webster in Dublin." He said the words slowly, his eyes intent upon her face.

She drew a deep breath. "Yes. I wrote to him about Katie."

His mouth curled in what was only the vaguest

of smiles. "So I see. Well, I felicitate you, my dear. Dr. Webster reports that your very helpful letters regarding her condition have at last convinced him he may be able to help her."

She felt a spark of triumph. "Oh, I knew he would!"

Avery's eyes narrowed slightly, but his face was still unreadably cool. "You appear to have been most persistent in your supplications to him."

She sighed. "Don't get in a pet, Avery. I know I should have discussed it with you, but I wanted to get his opinion first. I didn't want to get everyone's hopes up before I knew he was willing to help us."

He drew up one leg and stared down into the churchyard. When he spoke at last, the coolness in his voice had dropped to an icy politeness. "I thought, my dear, that I had already made it perfectly clear on several occasions that I do not wish for Katie to see any other doctor but Dr. Fitzgerald."

She laughed, not wishing to show him that his anger frightened her. "Well, it isn't as though I spirited her off and had some charlatan dose her up with false cures. I merely asked him his medical opinion."

"Against my express wishes."

She smiled her reproof against such melodrama, but he was not looking at her. "Avery, she is not the delicate baby she was when she was born. Look at her." She flung out her hand toward where Katie was shouting enthusiastically after her brother, who had managed to frighten the hare and was racing after it. "You cannot tell me she is too weak to bear Dr. Webster's treatment."

He turned to her, his eyes blazing. "Why has my

daughter's lameness always been an issue with you? Why can you not let her go on as she is?"

She would not let him see how much this accusation wounded her. "Really, Avery, you can't fly into a rage and pretend I do not care about your children. You know very well I would never allow anyone, doctor or not, to harm them. I am happy to drop the matter, if that is what both you and she wish. I only thought that I would look into options."

A muscle in the side of his mouth twitched. "Katie!" he called out. "Come over here."

The girl gave one last reluctant look at where Jane and Emmet were racing after the hare and then made her way back to her father.

"Gillian has written to a doctor who thinks he might be able to help straighten your leg. He is not certain if he can do anything and it might be a rather uncomfortable treatment for you. Do you wish to go see him?"

"Really?" Katie gave an incomprehensible squeak of joy and launched herself into her father's arms. "No crutch?"

"That would be the idea."

"Don't like crutch." She kicked it with the toe of her scuffed shoe.

"Are you certain?" He looked seriously down at his daughter. "It might take a long time, and it might not work, you know."

"Yes." Her blond brows drew together. "I hates my crutch. It ruins my princess dress." She settled more comfortably into his arms and smiled up at him as though the matter were entirely decided.

"Well." Avery looked up at Gillian, his face a mask of inscrutable civility. "I suspect we had better write Dr. Webster and tell him we are coming."

Chapter Eighteen

Avery threw another cravat into the trunk and scowled. Of course he could have let his valet pack, but it was infinitely more satisfying to go about banging drawers and flinging things. Plus, he would have the added benefit of getting annoyed all over again when he arrived in Dublin and found his clothes a hopelessly rumpled jumble.

How just like Gillian to go barging around doing things without telling him. Of course she thought she was doing it for the best. She always did, but it would have been nice to live in the belief that he still had some vestige of control over his family's future.

He flung a shirt across the room. It hit the lid of the trunk and then slumped down into the cavity. Gillian had even taken the children out to Elizabeth's grave without asking him. He ignored the prickles of guilt reminded him he should have been the one to plan the children's remembrance day.

He took up another shirt and prepared to throw it. It was the one Gillian had forbidden him to wear since he had stained the sleeve painting the model of King John's castle he and Emmet had built. He smoothed his hand across the front of it, remembering how she had sat with them, patiently holding the picture book and trying to subtly impart the more gory parts of the castle's history. He put the shirt on the bed. Perhaps if they were not receiving visitors, he could wear it in Dublin.

He was just working up his annoyance again when he saw the waistcoat she had embroidered for his birthday. It was a splendid affair in cream and two colors of green. She had worked on it for months in front of his oblivious eyes and smiled with a new kind of shyness at his praise when he received it. He added it to the pile. He couldn't very well leave it behind.

And there were the stockings with the clocks she particularly liked and the breeches he had worn when he escorted her to Almack's during the Season. There was the driving coat she had bought him there so they could cut a dash together in Hyde Park and the dressing gown he wore when he slipped through the connecting doors between their bedrooms. He folded its creases more carefully and gently placed the stack of clothes into the trunk.

Maybe Gillian was right. Maybe the doctor could fix Katie's foot. For the first time he allowed himself to imagine the girl running about with the other children. Pretty little Katie in her princess dress. He remembered the many evenings he had read aloud to Gillian while she made that dress. He

rubbed his suddenly stinging eyes and turned back
to the clothespress.

When Williams came to cord up the trunk, it
was filled nearly to overflowing. He looked at the
contents for a few moments, obviously struggling
to contain himself. "Milord?" he ventured when
he could stand it no longer. "Must we bring this?"
He held up a waistcoat between his thumb and
forefinger. "I know it was quite fashionable *last*
season . . ."

"My wife likes it," he said shortly.

"But *this* sir?" The valet dropped the waistcoat
to withdraw something even more horrifying from
the trunk. "It . . . it's *stained.*"

"Pollen." Avery smiled at the memory. "Lady
Avery leaned against me when she wore flowers in
her hair at the Needlings' ball." He shoved his
arm into his blue superfine coat sleeve. "Oh, there
is no need to look so horrified, Williams. I shan't
wear it."

"But—"

"Oh, I don't know. I just wanted to bring it."

"But—"

Avery buttoned his coat and jammed on his hat.
"Really, Williams. As much as I would truly enjoy
explaining my reasons for bringing every item in
that trunk, I find I am both unwilling and unable
to at the moment." He strode to the door and
opened it. "I suggest you get the offensive thing
out of your sight by cording it up and getting it
downstairs to load with the rest of the baggage."

He was turning into a sentimental fool. Gillian
would laugh herself silly if she knew of his little
collection. But she probably wouldn't even remember that she had once told him that she preferred
him in blue, since it matched his eyes.

He found himself strangely looking forward to their time in Dublin. Perhaps once he was away from this place, he would finally spend some time alone with her. In London she had managed to keep herself constantly busy with the children. How, when she had been with him all along in the past months, could he possibly tell her he had missed her?

As he picked his way through the mountains of luggage on the front steps, doubt assailed him. What if this was the wrong decision? Perhaps Dr. Webster could do nothing for Katie. He might be a charlatan, happy to prey on those who were desperate for hope.

"Hey there, men!" he shouted "Do you want to burst open that trunk? Handle it with a bit more care, if you please." The men who were loading the carriage meant to carry the servants and baggage looked contrite and went on with their work.

"The children will be ready in another moment, Avery. I'm sorry we have been slow." Gillian came out of the house buttoning her pelisse.

"We could have set off half an hour ago if it weren't for all these infernal trunks," he grumbled. "Really, Gillian, how long do you think we are going for?"

She smiled her new, tense smile. "Well, I thought the children would be more comfortable if they had their favorite toys. And you know how unpredictable the weather can be in the autumn. I thought it might be best to bring clothes for every eventuality."

He could not help but laugh at her consternation. "Perhaps I should remind you that we are going to Dublin, not China."

She absently tied her bonnet ribbons and looked behind her to see if the children were ready. "Are you certain you wish to do this, Avery? We can wait, you know. Dr. Webster said it is best to start young, but we can wait another year, if you would like."

He turned from her and pretended great interest in the stowage of yet another trunk. "We'll go now." The knot in his stomach was growing tighter.

She squinted doubtfully at the sky. "It will be slow going once that rain comes on."

"It will likely rain every day from now until Easter. There is no point in trying to avoid it."

She gave him a weak smile. "Yes, but there is little point in setting off in the middle of a rainstorm."

"It isn't raining yet," he pointed out. "And if this infernal luggage hadn't taken so long to load, we might have been well ahead of it."

"You know Katie was complaining of a headache last night. Perhaps we should postpone the trip if she is getting ill."

He opened the coach door and let the steps down. "For heaven's sake, next thing you'll be wringing your hands. We've made the decision to go, and Dr. Webster is expecting us."

She nodded at this gruff encouragement and helped the children into the carriage.

He had thought it would be a mistake to bring Janie and Emmet. After all, they would have been more comfortable at home with Bitsy, Mrs. Ahern, and Mrs. O'Connor looking after them. But Gillian insisted that for the children, comfort was more about being with their father than about being spared jouncing about in an exceedingly crowded traveling coach for days on end.

Perhaps she had been right. The children, provided by Gillian with all manner of books, puzzles, and drawing paper, were much more pleasant traveling companions than he had anticipated. Only once did Emmet contrive to get himself left behind at a coaching inn, and Katie, to her credit, confined herself to asking if they were there yet to only twice every quarter hour.

Furthermore, if Janie and Emmet had not come, it would have been only Katie and Gillian with him. He would have been expected to make conversation with Gillian. For days. And what was there to say?

"There seem to be quite a lot of nice things to do in Dublin," she said, closing up the guidebook she had been reading for the past hour.

He dragged his attention from where he had been watching the raindrops dribble down the window and found her eyes upon him. "Yes," he said shortly. "Though it is nothing to London."

"The children and I will have plenty to see, and perhaps you can meet up with some of your old friends from Trinity."

"Perhaps." He knew she was trying to make pleasant conversation, but he found he did not wish to talk. He could not shake off the feeling that she had goaded him into this trip against his better judgment. But was it better? Perhaps all along he had been cheating Katie out of a normal life through his autocratic pride.

"Even if Dr. Webster cannot help Katie, we will have a very nice holiday in Dublin, I think."

"Certainly." Perhaps at the next change, he would drive the horses for a while. That would blow the cobwebs from his brain and drive off his ill-tempered fidgets. He wished Gillian was not pressed quite so close against him in the crowded coach. It was stirring up completely unacceptable thoughts in his mind.

He closed his eyes and pretended to be asleep.

"Gilly," Katie said, sotto voce, "my head hurt."

Through his lashes, he saw his wife draw Katie onto her lap and press her cheek to the girl's forehead. "I'll make you a draught when we stop again to change horses." She spoke soothingly, but he saw a worried frown cross her face.

By the time they had reached the next coaching inn, there was little doubt that Katie was indeed quite ill. Her eyes were feverishly bright and heavy, and her cheeks were flushed.

"I'm sorry, Avery, but I really think we must stop for the night. I'm certain it is nothing, and she will be better by morning." Gillian smoothed Katie's white-blond hair as the girl lay draped over her shoulder.

"Of course. After I bespeak rooms for us, I will have a doctor sent for. Just to be certain."

Gillian looked up at him with an expression of relieved gratitude. It struck an odd pain in his chest. It had never occurred to him before that his self-sufficient, confident wife might actually want his help. When he went to stroke his daughter's cheek, his hand accidentally brushed his wife's shoulder, but she did not move away.

There were two rooms available, neither particularly fine, but he was in no mood to quibble over them. He did not bother taking off his greatcoat, but saw to it that Gillian and the children were deposited with the baggage before he struck out again to find a doctor. Of course, one of the servants could have been sent, but there was a feeling of anxiety like a spinning top in his chest that kept driving him to move rather than sit and wait for his orders to be carried out.

He felt bad leaving Gillian standing in the empty room with the trunks piled around her and Katie lying lethargically in her arms. Emmet had managed, in the two steps between the coach and the door of the inn, to fall face first into the mud. He was howling and dancing about, less hurt than annoyed that no one was paying him any mind. Janie was clinging to Gillian's hand and demanding querulously to know what was happening. He salved his guilt with the knowledge that Bitsy and the other servants would be arriving in the second coach soon.

The carriage horse he was forced to ride was anything but fleet of foot, but he arrived at last at the house the innkeeper had recommended. He strode up the path and pounded on the door.

The doctor, who was just sitting down to dinner when he barged in, loudly demanding his attention, did not seem disposed to come to the aid of an unknown gentleman whose daughter appeared to be suffering from nothing more than a cold. However, when he entered the room at the inn, propelled somewhat forcibly by Avery's hand at his elbow, his expression changed entirely.

"Get those other children out of here," he said sharply, as he opened up his case. "Do you want them all feverish? Here, let me see the child. When did the symptoms begin?"

Avery led Janie and Emmet out of the room. As he closed the door, he could hear Gillian's calm voice rise and fall as she answered the doctor's questions. He tried to quell the rising sense of urgency he felt by reminding himself that Gillian and the doctor were both far more qualified than he to deal with Katie.

In his throat he felt the same choking lump of panic as he had felt when he had closed the door on the doctor and Elizabeth.

"Papa, what is happening?" Janie asked for the ninth time.

He forced himself to grin. "Katie is ill. Most likely from eating too many of those sweets Gillian bought you in Nenagh. We'll soon have her right and tight. In the meantime, it's lashing down rain, so there's little point in going on tonight. I'll order up a bath for you, Emmet. Don't make that face at me, young cub. You're up to your eyebrows in mud. Bitsy will be here in a moment, and she will get you your dinner."

"But we can't go to sleep without a story from you and a song from Gilly," Janie protested.

"And I never have baths on Tuesdays!"

He ignored their protests and launched into an intricate and highly fallacious account of his adventures on the way to find the doctor.

"And after you fought off the bear, what happened?" Emmet demanded.

"Well . . . everything was going very well, until I came to a bridge. I was halfway across it when what do you think jumped out and blocked my path? A troll!" He cursed Bitsy for being so slow. What could the doctor have discovered in the next room? Something in the man's expression had sent a flash of fear through him.

At last the servant's carriage came rumbling into the stable yard. A few moments later, he heard Bitsy's graceless tread on the stairs, and she burst into the room.

"What's wrong with Miss Katie, milord?" she demanded breathlessly.

He stood up from where he was attempting to scrub some of the rapidly caking mud off of Emmet's face. "She merely has taken a chill, most likely," he replied, with a lightness he did not feel. "But Lady Avery is in with the doctor, just to be certain."

"Oh." Bitsy visibly relaxed. "Lady Avery will know just what to do."

Avery felt a strange surge of pride, mingled with something like envy. He had worried once that a woman could never truly care for children who were not her own flesh and blood. Instead, in those long days when he had been out riding, swathed in his own fog of lost love, Gillian had been teaching Janie to speak French, building battlefields with Emmet, and singing Katie that strange song about the baker's daughter who puffed up like yeast bread.

It was exactly what, a year ago, he had decided he wanted. He had a wife who raised his children lovingly and yet did not demand any such emotion from himself. But now he wondered if, in the excessive selfishness of grief, he had neglected them all. And they had gone on without him.

He crossed the hallway in two strides and slipped into the room where Katie lay on the bed. She looked very small, her body taking up only the first third of the coverlet. The strange, empty flatness at the foot of the bed disturbed him. His daughter lay quietly, but her face was still flushed and feverish. Gillian knelt beside her. Her traveling dress was inches deep in mud at the hem and her hair was coming down around her temples, but she did not seem to notice. The doctor stood over them like a shadow.

Gillian turned to him when she heard the door open. Her face was twisted into an expression of fear that cut through him like a blade.

"Avery," she said in a hoarse voice. "It's brain fever."

Chapter Nineteen

She should have broken the news to him with more care. For a moment he only stared at her with a stricken face and glazed eyes.

"Brain fever," he repeated dully.

"An inflammation of the meninges that cover the brain," the doctor provided, somewhat unhelpfully. "I have provided her with a draught to ease her pain, but . . ."

In a step he had closed in on the doctor. "But what?" he demanded. "What can you do for her?"

"It is an extremely serious illness," the man said, undaunted by Avery's menacing proximity. "We must hope for the best." He turned and began repacking his belongings into his bag. "I will come back in the morning. I have left a second draught with your wife to be administered in six hours."

Gillian thought for a moment that Avery would choke the man.

"You're leaving?" His voice rose to an unseemly level and his hands twitched at his sides. "You take a half hour to make a diagnosis of my child and then you leave her? What kind of charlatan are you? Brain fever, indeed. I doubt you have the slightest notion of what you are talking about."

The doctor tiredly put on his hat. His eyes drifted to Gillian, where she still knelt at the side of the bed. "Shall I have the innkeeper send up your dinner?" He turned back to Avery. "And a drink?"

Avery ran a hand through his hair. "I will ride to the next town, Gillian. I'll get another doctor." His gestures were growing frantic. "A doctor who knows what he is about. One who won't leave Katie like this. One who won't say—"

"Avery," she cut him off. "There is nothing to be done but wait. I would rather Katie fight off the illness with us watching over her than a pack of strangers. Dr. Hayes has done all he can."

That man took the opportunity to bow himself out of the room. Avery stared at the closed door for a moment and then turned back to her. He took her hands and held them tightly. She could see in his eyes that he was afraid.

"Brain fever," he whispered, the words catching roughly in his throat.

She nodded and turned back to the bed. Katie's eyes were half closed, but they moved between herself and Avery. She smoothed the girl's damp hair. "I feel certain he is correct. But your Katie's a fine, strong girl. She'll pull through for her Papa." She smiled encouragingly at him, but he did not seem to see her.

He dragged a chair over to her bedside and hunched down to look into his daughter's face.

"How are you doing, my poppet?" The ache in his voice was painful to hear.

"Head hurt," she said fretfully. "Blanket too hot."

Gillian stood up. "I'll go and get some cool water and a cloth." It would be best to give them some time alone. There was every chance Avery would lose his daughter tonight—the daughter that had cost him Elizabeth. The pain she felt for him was almost unbearable.

"Send a servant for it," he said quickly. "Katie needs you here."

She gave him a smile she hoped was reassuring, but he had already turned back toward the bed. She rang for someone and then pulled up a chair beside his. The serving girl came and went, returned with the water, and left them again, but still he said nothing.

Gillian twisted the water out of the cloth and patted it across Katie's face. She had fallen into a light, fitful sleep that seemed to take more strength from her than it gave relief. Avery sat silent, his hand playing with his daughter's limp fingers.

When the dinner tray came up, he tried to spoon some broth between the girl's lips, but she would only cry and say it hurt to move her head.

For hours she was content only with being held and walked about the small room. Gillian sat and watched with an aching heart as Avery trod a slow circuit around the room. He walked carefully so as not to jar her, his long, fine fingers ceaselessly stroking her hair. The night dragged on, with both father and daughter growing more drawn and exhausted.

Then, when Katie became restless and fretful, Gillian took her on her lap and rocked her, quietly

singing every song she knew until her voice was
hoarse. Avery stood silent and anxious over them
both. When she had finally sung out her repertoire,
they sat in silence, ceaselessly rocking and
watching.

At last he put her back in the tousled bed and
resumed his seat beside his wife. Katie's sleeping
face was flushed. Her pale eyebrows and lashes
stood out in strange, milky contrast.

Avery did not take his eyes off her, but he did
not object when Gillian pulled off his coat, poured
him a cup of tea, and gently rubbed his neck and
shoulders.

"It is time for her second draught, but I don't
want to wake her," she whispered. She hadn't used
her voice in so long, it came out strangely rusty.

"Do you think we should wait a bit? She's only
now dropped off."

It was touching that he would look to her for
advice and crushing that she should not know the
answer. What had ever given him to think she knew
the first thing about raising children? Of course,
in the last year she had learned any number of
things about baths and sulks and picky eating habits, but this? This was worse than anything she had
imagined. And she was completely unqualified.

Katie's eyelids fluttered open. "Where is Jane
and Emmet?" she asked urgently, trying to drag
the coverlet off of her.

"Bitsy put them to bed. You will sleep here tonight. With Gillian and me to watch over you."
Avery pushed the coverlet away and pulled the
sheet over her. "Is that better?"

"I don't want sleep. My head hurt."

"But you must try to lie quietly."

"I want Molly."

He looked up at Gillian with an expression of panic.

"Her doll," she explained. She turned to Katie. "She's packed up in a trunk. Would you feel better if I went and found her for you?"

"But Molly lost. Lost all her hair. She fell in the river." There was a strange singsong combination of fear and resignation in Katie's voice. "And Aunt Louisa cross acause you told a story about it."

Gillian and Avery exchanged anxious glances. "She is delirious," she said softly.

"Where is Gilly? I want Gilly."

"I'm here, my dear."

Katie looked at her with unseeing eyes and continued to call out for her.

"Does that mean she is worse?"

Avery looked at her with an expression of helplessness that made her long to fling her arms around him and assure him she felt the same fears. Instead, she stood up and went again to the pitcher of water. "I think she must be."

He held the girl while Gillian made her drink the doctor's draught. She wet the cloth and began the process of cooling Katie's forehead. Avery was quiet for a moment, carefully wiping away the water that dripped from the cloth with his fingers. "Elizabeth was delirious before she died." His words were thoughtful, as though he were speaking aloud to himself.

She turned the cloth over, ran her fingers through Katie's curls, and sat down again beside her husband. Her own head ached from exhaustion and strain. Whatever pain she might feel must be nothing to his own grief. He was having to relive the agony of watching Elizabeth slip from him in a fever by watching the same thing happen to his youngest child. A feeling of helplessness washed over her. There was nothing she could do for Katie and nothing she could do for Avery.

"Children are very resilient," she said at last, trying to inject encouragement into her voice. "It may not be as dire as Dr. Hayes said."

"Yes, of course." His eyes were on his daughter's fever-flushed face. "You always maintained that Katie was a good deal stronger than the rest of us gave her credit for."

She turned her face to the uncurtained window where she could see the reflection of the two of them in their macabre tableau. She did not want him to see how badly his words had hurt her. "I know you blame me, Avery," she said in a tight voice. "You said she was too frail to make this trip and I said she wasn't. I know, no matter what happens, this is my fault."

His hand gripped the back of her neck so suddenly she flinched. "Gillian," he said passionately. "I never meant it that way. You could not have foreseen this. I never—" He forced her to turn her face to his and looked down at her with blazing eyes. "I know you only want what's best for Katie."

She clenched her teeth to keep the tears back. The last thing he needed was to deal with a hysterical wife. "It's true, Avery, you know that." She clenched her hands in her lap. "I love her. I love them all. Like . . . like they were my own."

His hand covered her fists. "I know," he said softly. He guided her head to his shoulder and ran his hand through the curls at the nape of her neck with a gesture as tender as that he had used with Katie. "I need someone to lean against me," he said softly, recalling the time they had sat together in the stables on Christmas. It seemed like so long ago. But as she had then, she drew strength from his closeness.

His chest lifted and fell in a sigh. "You are much better in these times of crisis than I am. Don't look so surprised, my dear. Do you recall when Emmet broke his nose? You were so calm and collected. You took care of everything. I would have sat there in paralyzed terror while he bled to death."

"Oh, he wouldn't have bled to death," she objected prosaically, her voice muffled against his shoulder. She felt a sort of dreamy peace when he held her. The smell of his linen and his skin beneath it reminded her of those intimate times she had tried to push from her mind.

He reached out and brushed a lock of hair off Katie's forehead. The girl moved away from his hand and murmured something unintelligible.

"Elizabeth could not stand illness or unpleasantness. She saw Katie only once before she died. She was horrified by the baby's twisted foot."

"She would have grown to love her. How could anyone help it?"

"Perhaps," he conceded. "But she would not have known what to do in a situation like this."

She took a corner of the sheet between her fingers and smoothed it. "I don't believe any of us know what to do right now."

The fire on the grate died down to a flicker that finally went out entirely. The embers dimmed and whitened to ash as the sky paled along the horizon. They continued to sit, watching Katie as she breathed. Gillian still sat with her head on her husband's shoulder. His own chest rose and fell in time with his daughter's. She wondered if he had fallen asleep. She shifted to press her hand against Katie's forehead. It seemed cooler, but her own hands had grown cold in the night, so it was difficult to assess the fever's progress. She turned to see Avery's eyes upon her.

"I'm glad you're here with me, Gillian," he said quietly.

It seemed like the day had broken hours ago when the doctor clumped slowly up the stairs to the little room, but it was only seven o'clock. Gillian and Avery stood up and made room for him at the bedside. Gillian expected her husband to snap at him and demand why it had taken him so long to check in on his little patient, but he stood silent, an anxious look on his face.

"I hear the child slept some in the night," Dr. Hayes said gruffly, by way of greeting. He swept off his hat and opened his bag without taking his eyes off Katie.

She began to cry when he took her wrist, but when she saw her father and Gillian still standing by the bed, she quieted somewhat. She looked alarmed at the doctor's gruff questions, but managed to answer them rationally. Gillian rubbed her aching forehead. At least the girl seemed to have regained her wits. Surely that must be a good sign. Her hand found Avery's and pressed it.

The doctor cleared his throat. "I do not wish to raise your hopes too high in a matter so delicate." He scowled. "But the danger seems to have passed for the time being."

The breath she didn't realize she had been holding rushed out of her lungs. She sagged slightly. Katie was out of danger. Avery would not look at her and think that her ambitious desire to help his daughter walk had been the cause of her death. The doctor continued talking but the buzzing in her ears blocked out his words. Katie would not die. Everything would be all right. After a long moment she realized both Avery and the doctor were staring at her.

"Madam, are you unwell?" The doctor's face loomed up in front of her.

"No, of course not. I'm fine. I'm just relieved." Her voice sounded like it came from somewhere outside her body. She was glad to find Avery was supporting her, for her knees seemed suddenly wobbly.

"Does your neck hurt?"

What a strange question. She tried to collect her fuzzy thoughts. "Well, yes, but I have been sitting in an awkward position for hours. It is merely a kink. I assure you . . ."

Avery's arm around her tightened. The irritation she felt at being made much of when the doctor should have been paying attention to Katie was rapidly waning to apathy.

"She's caught it," she heard the doctor say in a low voice.

Did the man think she couldn't hear? "Of course not," she snapped. "Don't be ridiculous." She rubbed her stinging eyes. "Please look after Katie. I am merely tired."

But the doctor had turned back to his bag and was mixing up another draught. "You can have another bed set up in here. Don't let the other children in. I'm afraid you shouldn't go and see them, either, or you'll likely infect them, too. Your little girl won't be harmed by it, as she already has it. You and I," he smiled his grim smile, "will have to take our chances."

She couldn't have caught it. Not when Avery needed her to help nurse Katie. And what about Janie and Emmet? They couldn't be left alone with only Bitsy to mind them. "Really, Dr. Hayes, I must insist . . ."

Avery forced her into a chair and went to ring for a servant. Katie was beginning to set up a feeble crying. A rather frantic knocking on the door turned out to be Bitsy, in hysterical tears because she had forgotten to pack any of Emmet's clothes. Behind the nursemaid, she could hear Janie demanding to know what was going on and insisting her father be sent to her immediately. The doctor forced a glass of liquid into Gillian's hand.

Avery shut the door in Bitsy's face and went back to jerk the bell for the servant. Katie's crying grew louder. He ran his hand through his hair in a gesture of extreme frustration.

Just when everything was looking better. Just when everything could return to normal. She turned to him in anguish. "Oh, Avery, I'm so sorry."

Chapter Twenty

Avery wrung out the cloth and passed it over his own forehead. He wondered tiredly if he himself were feverish, but found he didn't really care. He braced his arms on the washstand and drew a deep breath.

"Prescott, you're being foolish," Gillian said quietly. "Lie down and get some rest."

He poured out fresh water and crossed the room to where she lay in bed. Her skin was fiercely hot to the touch, but he tried not to show his fear. Outside he could hear the sounds of carriages in the inn yard and the shouts of the hostlers. It must be quite far into the day, but it was hard to tell. The rain continued to pour down and the room seemed sunk in a perpetual, timeless gloom. He felt strangely as though he had never done anything else in his life but this. The eternal circuit: Katie, water, Gillian, water.

"You cannot go on like this." She tried to push his hand away.

"Nonsense," he said with a cheer he did not feel. "Who better to nurse the two of you? I've already been exposed, and there is little sense in running the risk of having Bitsy or one of the other servants come down with it. We should start a never-ending cycle of people collapsing with the fever."

She smiled weakly at this attempt at levity. "But you were up all last night and all of today. There is a limit to what one can endure."

He laid the cloth across her forehead, trying to ignore the fear that whirled in his chest when he looked at her heavy eyes. They both knew the course of the illness well by now. In a few more hours, the fever would reach its peak.

"How could I sleep with Katie whining all day?" He glanced at his daughter, who was now placidly engaged in looking at a picture book. "I feel like I've been boarded up in a plague house with the two of you." He roughly twitched Gillian's blanket up closer to her chin. "And worse patients I've never seen, with Katie fractious and you plaguing me to leave off cosseting you and take care of her."

"Well, you should." She scowled. There was a whiteness around her mouth and lines of tension across her forehead that made him uneasy.

"Katie is getting better," he said with mock severity.

"Papa, drink. Me wants water," that personage demanded imperiously from her throne of pillows. "And a story." She jabbed her finger at the book. "Me wants a story."

Gillian smiled faintly. "And I am worse."

"Don't be melodramatic, my dear," he said lightly, going to pour Katie her glass of water. Gillian was right; she was worse. Much worse. She had hidden it as long as she could, foolishly harboring some guilt for being troublesome. But it had become clear upon the doctor's second visit that his wife would be in for a fight even more desperate than Katie's. He fought down the feeling of nausea at the thought of what tonight might hold.

"Gilly sick now, too," Katie said sympathetically. "Everybody sick." She took the glass of water and shoved the book into his hand. "Gilly need a story."

He took the book and settled back into the chair by the fire. "Very well, I will read Gilly a story. But you must not listen, Katie, because it isn't for you."

"Papa!" she protested with a giggle.

"Yes, yes, I will read you both a story." He opened the book and frowned. "But this book has no words, Katie. It is only pictures."

"Gilly tells story from pictures," Katie informed him, with a disparaging look that reminded him disconcertingly of Louisa.

He shot a glance at Gillian. Her eyes were closed, but a smile twitched at the corners of her lips.

"Ah. Well. Let's see here. Once upon a time there was a little boy—"

"Girl!" Katie interrupted "It's a little girl! Named Katie."

"Right. Of course that is what I meant. A little girl named Katie. She lived in a very beautiful forest with a lot of charming little animals who looked rather as though they might be hedgehogs." He glanced at Katie, but she seemed to find this satisfactory. "And one day—"

"Names, Papa! Tell me their names!"

"Names?" He looked at Gillian, but she seemed to have fallen genuinely asleep.

"Willy and Nilly and Fractious and Frumpus and

Higgle and Piggle and Ted," Katie provided with an impatient scowl.

"Ah. Yes, of course those were their names. And let's see. On the next page it looks like—"

"Papa! Fractious says, 'Why don't we have rout party?'"

"Oh, Katie, I don't know this story very well."

"No," she said severely. "You don't."

He handed the book back to her. "Why don't you read it to Gillian? She would like that, I know."

Katie sighed. "Yes. I think I will have to."

Avery, finding himself unable to sit still, went back to check on Gillian. Her breathing was shallow, but she lay quietly. In a way he wished she wouldn't. There was something about her stillness and pallor that was far too much like death. What would he do if he lost her? No, he wouldn't think about that. It would drive him to madness.

Katie launched into a rambling, hedgehog-riddled account of a rout party. At least the girl seemed better. She had spent a fretful day and was still weak, but her natural buoyancy had returned, and though her recovery was likely to be slow, there was every reason to suppose it would be complete. The doctor had seemed well satisfied with her progress.

When he had looked at Gillian, however, his grave face had sagged into even more dour lines. He made no prognosis, but merely gave a few terse orders to the servants and left his customary draughts.

"Papa! Are you listening?"

"Of course, poppet."

"Are you, Gilly?"

"She's asleep, my dear." He brushed his hand across Gillian's hot forehead. Would she grow delirious tonight? The idea filled him with dread. If he had to watch her suffer, please let it be after Katie had gone to sleep. How could he explain to her what Gillian was going through? She would think her stepmama was dying. Which she might well be, a grim voice in his head reminded him.

Katie had lost interest in the book and had sunk back against the pillows. She looked tired, but softly, almost under her breath, she was singing the song about the baker's daughter. Avery turned away from her so she would not see the expression on his face.

How could his children stand to lose their mother and now Gillian? Katie, once again, might be spared understanding, but for Emmet and Janie the devastation would be worse. He thought of them across the hall, closed out of the sick room, just like before.

He looked at the slips of paper that littered Gillian's coverlet. Knowing they would feel left out and anxious, she had spent the day exchanging silly notes with them. Emmet's missives generally contained a few wobbly words and lurid drawings depicting his misadventures in the stables, the subsequent chase through the kitchen, Bitsy's expression when she caught him, and the dessert he had cruelly been forced to forgo.

Janie's careful handwriting primly expressed her best wishes for the recovery of the patients and dolefully prophesied that without proper guidance, her brother would come to a bad end. There was one note that Gillian still held crumpled in her limp hand. He knew which one it was. The one that had arrived last, before the children had been put to bed.

Dear Gilly,

*I wish we could see you, but Bitsy says we mustn't.
I wouldn't care if I caught the fever from you,
because I can't bear being without you and Papa.
I heard the doctor say that you were very ill and
might die like Mama. Emmet hit him and said it
wasn't true. Please say it isn't. Once, when you first
came, I wished you had died and Mama had lived.
I don't wish that anymore. Please get well.*

*Love,
Jane Avery*

Postscript: And if you die, I will never learn French.

He and Gillian had laughed over Janie's prim
signature and horrifyingly prosaic postscript, but
she had not let the letter out of her hand.

There was another letter. When he had helped
her into her nightclothes, he had found it. Between
her gown and her chemise was tucked that old,
worn letter he had found on her writing desk so
long ago. It had fallen to the floor, limp with age
and many readings. She had swept it up and put
it with her things without a word.

Now he retrieved it from where she had tucked
it between the folds of her discarded gown and
looked it over again. What would he say if he were
to write her now? He likely wouldn't be more articu-
late, but somehow, again, perhaps she would know
his sentiments. He refolded the letter and slid it
under her pillow. "And you told me once you were
not romantic," he said softly.

For a moment, the fierce joy he felt almost over-
powered the fear.

Katie fell asleep at last. He made certain she was
comfortable and then went back to sitting by his

wife. Gillian's breathing was quick and labored. The crescent of her dark lashes was echoed by heavy circles under her eyes. All day she had struggled to minimize her symptoms, and he had almost believed that her case was milder than Katie's. But now, with all her animation stilled, he could see in her sunken cheeks that it had all been a sham.

It was all too horrifyingly familiar. A woman lying immobile in bed and himself, helpless, his heart being pulled apart inside him. He again wrung out the cloth and applied it to Gillian's neck and arms.

He thought of that night three years ago. He had been allowed to take Katie in to show Elizabeth. She had cried at the sight of the girl's leg and refused to look at her again. Then the surgeon had arrived to let his wife's blood, and he was turned out of the room. His first love, his childhood sweetheart, and they had hustled him out like a stranger. He had never even had the chance to say good-bye to her.

At least now he was doing something. Futile, perhaps, but at least it gave him the illusion of control. And it kept his mind off the constant, awful refrain in the back of his mind: Gillian could die.

He took a strand of her hair and wound it around his finger. "You weren't what I expected," he said softly. "You weren't what I thought I wanted. I wanted someone mild and sweet. Someone like Elizabeth. You came in and turned everything upside down."

He felt rather foolish talking aloud, but somehow these were things he needed to say. He smiled bitterly. Things that should have been said long ago. Even now he had the courage to speak them aloud only when she was asleep.

"My world needed to be turned upside down. The children needed someone just like you, someone who would play with them and who wouldn't be bullied by them. I worried so much that you would not be able to feel real affection for them. I never thought about what you needed."

He caught up her hot, dry hand and pressed it to his cheek. "I spent so much time buried in selfish grief. And even once that had faded, I was too guilty, too ashamed to admit to myself that I had fallen in love with you. I felt that to admit that you made me happy, that you made me feel more alive than I ever felt in my life, would be disrespectful to Elizabeth." His voice was hoarse. "You fulfill needs I never even knew I had."

He was glad now that she could not see him. What a great babbling sentimental fool she would think her husband. He pressed a kiss on her fingers.

"And I am still selfish. I need you, and I don't want to lose you. I won't let you go. I want to spend the rest of my life learning about you and finding a way to make you love me as I love you."

She continued to sleep, fighting for every breath. He realized that he had somehow thought if he said the magic words, she would open her eyes like a fairy princess and tell him everything would be all right. He hunched miserably over her bed. One couldn't be given a second chance at life and love just to have it snatched away as well. It shouldn't happen that way.

Gillian wouldn't have just sat there, paralyzed with grief. She would have done something, anything rather than maudlinly assume the worst was inevitable. He stood and went to ring for more water. Perhaps there was nothing to be done, but he couldn't let her slip away while he did nothing.

All his life he had hated conflict. Neither he nor Elizabeth could deal with unpleasantness. But Gillian faced life head-on. Clear-eyed and cool-headed, she was never one to flinch from reality.

He kissed her on the mouth, a new and resolute strength filling him. "No, my dear, you are nothing if not determined. And I will not let you give up. If love and pure bullheadedness can make you well, you shall be in very good hands indeed."

"Yes," she whispered. "I know."

Chapter Twenty-one

Gillian lay staring at the ceiling for quite a long time before she recalled where she was and why she felt so terrible. She tried to sit up, but a gentle hand pushed her back onto the pillow.

"Welcome back." Avery smiled.

It all came flooding back to her. The inn. Katie. But the bed across the room was empty. Panic tore through her. "What time is it? Where is Katie? What has happened?"

To her dismay, her husband laughed. "She is having a bath. She is very much better. You are the one who has worried us." She saw now that despite his smile, he had the pale and drawn look of someone who has spent too many days and nights awake and indoors. He must have seen her bewildered look. "It is now Friday night. You've lost a good three days."

She started at him, horrified. "Three days?"

He took her hand and pressed it to his lips in a gesture that seemed to come as naturally to him as it was strange to her. "I'm afraid so. I was treated to several rather remarkable conversations during your delirium, but mostly I'm sorry to report that you were a dead bore."

"Oh." This seemed to be a lot to take in at once. And it was made stranger still by the fact that Avery was looking at her with the most peculiar expression. A rather horrifying suspicion assailed her. "What was I talking about?"

His grin was slow and wide. "Mostly about a horse named Butterfly."

She gave a rueful but relieved laugh. "Is that all? Well, I'm sorry you were forced to listen to my nonsense. It must have been very trying for you. But if you hadn't cast yourself as nurse . . ."

"And you mentioned something about ice skating."

"Did I? How odd. Well, I—"

"And you told me that you loved me. More than anything in the world." He looked boyishly delighted, almost expectant.

She felt a flush throb in her head. She had not planned to tell him. Perhaps ever. Surely things would have bobbed along as comfortably as they always had without any need to unburden her heart. "Yes," she said with a rueful smile. "I do. I think I always have."

"You love me," he repeated, relishing the words.

"It doesn't change anything," she said quickly. "Please don't feel you are obliged—"

"It makes things much easier," he interrupted.

"Why?" His expression was making her feel rather squirmy. In another moment she would be flinging herself into his arms and disgracing herself.

To her surprise, he leaned over and kissed her on the lips. "Because then I will not have to go to the trouble of *making* you fall in love with me."

When he released her at last, she lay back against the pillow, limp with confusion. "I feel like I missed a vital scene in a play."

He drew his long fingers across her cheek. "I suppose, in a way, you did. I had a lot of time to think while you were ill. And make no mistake, you were gravely ill indeed." He straightened the covers around her and smoothed the pillow with a tender gesture. He seemed to think of something, then reached under the pillow and pulled out a piece of paper.

"My letter." She reached out for it. "I would have been so upset if it were lost."

To her surprise, he kissed her passionately on the forehead. "I will write you a hundred more."

"I'm rather sentimental about this one," she said, rather needlessly.

He took it from her fingers and put it carefully on the table beside the bed. "It gave me hope, you know. Because you treasured it, it gave me hope you could love me."

"I do," she said simply. "I think I always have. Ever since you sent it to me. You sounded like you knew me. Like you were lonely and you needed me."

He gave her a rueful smile. "I wish I could take credit for being so enlightened." He stroked her hair for a long moment, absorbed in thought. "I did you a disservice by marrying you." He silenced her objections with a finger to her lips. "I had not finished grieving for Elizabeth. And I clung to that grief for much longer than I should have." He twisted the cloth of the coverlet between his finger for a long moment. "She was a good person, and I will never regret the time we had together. Tha time is gone. Now there is you." His mouth twisted into a smile that was somehow shy and triumphant "And you are everything."

"I know I can never replace her, Avery."

"I do not wish for you to," he said frankly. He leaned on the bed with one elbow and smiled a her. "With you I have fun. I have silly romps with the children and dancing on the lawn. I like being married to you."

She drew a deep breath and pressed her cheel into the crook of his arm. "Perhaps I am still deliri ous. Or"—she opened one eye and looked a him—"perhaps *you* are falling ill with the brain fever."

He dropped a kiss into her hair. "Yes, too much time with a very bad-tempered little invalid and her nonsensically babbling stepmother has made me hopelessly love struck."

She smiled happily up at him. "I make no com plaint."

The door opened and Bitsy brought Katie in She looked pale and a little thinner, but from her vociferous objections to being carried, her health seemed to have much improved. The little gir looked anxiously up at her father. "Gilly is better?"

Avery took her from Bitsy and swung her around "Much better, poppet. I shall let you tell Dr. Hayes so when he comes for his visit. Bitsy, will you tel Janie and Emmet that Gillian is awake and feeling much better?. I'll be in to see them myself in a moment."

When they neared the bed, Katie reached ou

her arms to Gillian. Avery transferred her to her stepmother's side. "I like Dr. Hayes," Katie confided, once she was settled on the bed next to her. "He makes funny faces."

Gillian couldn't imagine anything Dr. Hayes did as being amusing, but she raised no objection. Avery cautioned his daughter not to be too rambunctious and then slipped out to see his other children.

"How are you feeling, my dear?" she asked.

"Cross," the girl replied cheerfully. "But sick people are cross, and I very sick. You sick, too. Papa was very worried. But he can't be cross, only us."

She kissed Katie on the forehead. "I'm so happy to see you better, I don't believe I will ever be cross again."

The girl gave her a doubtful glance. "You don't know what Emmet did."

The door exploded open and Janie and Emmet launched themselves toward the bed.

"Don't bounce," Avery called out. "I'm sorry, Dr. Hayes, I should have warned them not to be so affectionate. But it has been so long since they have seen her."

Dr. Hayes' face contorted into what might, with only the greatest generosity, be called a smile. "I think the danger is past. The recovery will be slow, of course. No jaunting about for either of them for quite a while. However, you can, perhaps, plan to journey home in a week or so."

"Or to Dublin," Avery prompted him.

Gillian looked up at her husband from where she was pinned to the bed by three wiggly bodies who were all trying to get her attention at once.

"Dublin? But surely you cannot wish to continue that scheme. Katie has been so ill."

"She will recover just as well in Dublin as at home." He crossed the room and took her hand. "Dr. Hayes and I have had more opportunity for conversation than perhaps he would have liked. He agrees with you, Gillian. Something can be done for Katie, and it is best that we start when she is young. This illness was unfortunate, but, as you can see, she is recovering very well. It will take some time, but she was never as frail as I worried she might be. There is no reason to think there will be any deleterious effects from Dr. Webster's treatment."

"I believe, with a cautious approach, she is a good candidate for his new methods." Hayes plucked several children out of the way and leaned over to examine her. "You'll be all right, Lady Avery," he said gruffly. "Luckily you had the most devoted of nurses." He carefully extracted Emmet from his medical bag and divested him of various lethally sharp instruments. "And," he said in doleful accents, "a most loving family."

"Really, Lady Avery," Lady Edgecott said severely, "I don't know what you were thinking, going to Dublin. Amongst strangers at your time of need! You should have come immediately back to Glensharrold House. I would have tended to you and Katie myself."

Gillian closed her eyes and smiled up at the sun. "You're very kind to say so. But we managed very well in Dublin. There was nothing to do but rest, and I'm afraid we were extremely difficult patients. Poor Avery, we sorely tried him, I'm afraid." She looked across the lawn to where her husband was crouched at the edge of the pond, his three children clustered around him.

It was a beautiful autumn day. A day when there seemed that there could be nothing wrong in the world, and there was nothing to do but move the drawing room chairs out onto the lawn and spend the day alfresco.

"Poor Katie." Louisa shook her head. "I'll tell you plainly, my dear, I think she is worse off than before."

As they watched, Katie stood up awkwardly and peered into her cupped hands. She and Emmet studied the contents with interest. She did not seem to notice the metal and leather brace strapped to her leg.

"We waited a full month in Dublin until we were quite certain Katie was recovered before we had her fitted for the brace," Gillian replied. "Dr. Webster assured us she was quite well enough to embark on the treatment."

Louisa smoothed the hair of her youngest son, who sat beside her chair, sedately winding embroidery floss onto a card. "She looks like some kind of hideous machine. How could you put that sweet child into a contraption like that?"

"She can walk now," Gillian pointed out. "And in a few years she may be able to get on without it."

"Yes," her sister-in-law conceded, with an attempt at a frown that was not entirely successful. "And of course Dr. Fitzgerald is as mad as fire at your success. I never did like him, you know. He pooh-poohed my mustard plaster."

"Oh dear," Gillian replied mildly. "Perhaps we should contact the College of Physicians. A pooh-

pooh of that magnitude, and he should not be allowed to practice."

Lady Edgecott hid her laugh behind her teacup. "Really, my dear, you're as bad as Prescott."

"Is my wife bad?" Avery asked, coming across the lawn to them.

"Incorrigible," his sister informed him. "What were you doing down there that was so interesting?"

He flung himself down on the grass at Gillian's feet. "Emmet found a little fish lurking in the mud. Katie and he were in favor of taking it apart to see how it breathed in the water, but fortunately, Jane and I spoke on the fish's behalf." He looked up at his wife and laughed. "I suppose we will be looking for books on fishes now."

Jane bounded across the grass. She dropped a quick curtsey to her aunt and turned to Gillian. "Gilly, can we float Emmet's boat on the pond? We'll tie a string to it so it won't float off like last time. You can come too, George," she added generously.

Louisa looked horrified. "George cannot. He would catch influenza if he went near the water at this time of year."

"Mama . . ." He looked up at her pleadingly.

"It is very warm today," Gillian ventured. "And Bitsy could make certain he has the proper clothes."

"Oh, go on." She gestured tiredly. "But when he's coughing his poor lungs out, I shall lay it at your door." She watched Jane and her cousin go racing back to the house for the boat. "She is much improved," she said in a thoughtful tone. "They all are. Not the least you, Prescott."

"Oh yes, I'm entirely without fault now," Avery

replied with an impertinent grin. "My wife assures me of it."

Louisa shot him a look of doubt. "Perhaps the children's trip to Dublin did them good," she continued. "I still think Jane is a good deal too young for a governess, but I suppose Bitsy has her hands full with the other two. Really, I think sometimes Bitsy is most unsuitable as a nursemaid. She's far too young, you know. Emmet will be too much for her soon enough. He is as wild as a savage." She held her bonnet on her head and turned to look up at the sun. After a moment of silence, she sighed. "It was not the same without you here."

Avery leaned up against Gillian's knees and sighed in contentment. "She missed us, my dear," he said with a mischievous smile. "Just think of how lonely her life has been without anyone to badger and harass. Though I suspect Neil's wife Selina has borne the brunt of her advice."

His sister granted him a thin smile. "Exactly. I do not envy your keeping my brother in rein, Lady Avery. He is a good deal too much prone to levity these days."

Gillian slid her fingers through her husband's curls. "Entirely so." She closed her eyes again and enjoyed the golden autumn sunlight. "Do you know what today is?" she asked, after a long moment. Avery and his sister looked at her, puzzled. "One year ago today I was driving down that road on the way to meet my new husband."

Lady Edgecott's eyebrows rose. "Has it been only a year? I suppose it must have been. Well, a good deal has happened since then." She looked at Gillian with a slightly quizzical expression. "It must have been rather uncomfortable to inherit a husband and children secondhand."

"I cannot imagine my life any other way than it is right now," she said quietly. "And I would not want it any other way."

Avery kissed her on the knee and then looked up at her. "You do not still feel you are an outsider, do you?" He was smiling, but there was a faint shadow of doubt in his eyes.

She smoothed her fingers across his broad forehead to still the frown that was forming there. "I may have received my family ready-made, but they are still my family."

"Yes," Louisa said darkly. "And you will doubtless spoil them all useless."

Gillian looked down at her husband and smiled. "Undoubtedly."

ABOUT THE AUTHOR

Catherine Blair lives in New York. She is currently working on her next Zebra Regency romance, A PERFECT MISMATCH, which will be published in March, 2002. Catherine loves to hear from readers, and you may write to her c/o Zebra Books. Please include a self-addressed stamped envelope if you wish a response.

More Zebra Regency Romances